# PRAISE FOR BLACKWATER POND

## BOOK ONE: BENEATH AND BEYOND

Brian will tempt the mysterious pond. "Beneath and Beyond" is the first entry into the Blackwater Pond series as Brian chooses to pursue his missing brother to the pond and finds that what lurks within the pond awaits to challenge everything he thought he knew about it. A tale of fantasy and adventure, "Beneath and Beyond" is a fine pick for young adult fiction collections.

*–Midwest Book Review*

As a hard-core fan of all books fantasy, Stricklen did an awesome job portraying the adventures of curious teenage boys. It has all the potential of an epic triology in the making: romance, adventure, mystery, action, mystical creatures, and magical lands. An ingenious and original plot with unexpected twists and turns.

-Andrew J. Rosolino, Amazon.com Review

## BOOK TWO: THROUGH THE EYES OF THE BEAST

This book is GREAT! You won't be able to put it down. I read it, and then read it to my daughter and her friends. We all loved it! It takes you from this world to another world that is strange and mystical. There's one adventure after another. Even when you think everything is fine - it isn't! Great for young and old!

-Robin Crossman, Amazon.com Review

I enjoyed the underlying message of this coming-of age-story. Having teenage protagonists learn to think for themselves and the relationships they formed because of that could have easily become cliché, but the setting was so unique and their dialog so genuine, it never seemed the least trite. I'm excited that book 3 is in the works.

-Allison Marek, Amazon.com Review

# THROUGH THE EYES OF THE BEAST

## BOOK TWO OF BLACKWATER POND

*Best Wishes (with very few misses)*

*David S[...]*

### DAVID STRICKLEN

Through the Eyes of the Beast

Beachhead Publishing

Beachhead Publishing
2455 Norcrest Dr.
Norton Shores, MI 49441

Manufactured by Color House Graphics, Inc.,
Grand Rapids, Michigan, USA
July 2012
Job #37836

ISBN 978-1-4675-3581-6

# DEDICATION

I would like to dedicate Through the Eyes of the Beast to all the people who said, "Hey, where is the next book?" You know who you are. This encouragement lit a fire that helped propel me into the second adventure.

I would also like to give special thanks to my wife Cheryl and my great boys Justin and Jordan. Cheryl and Jordan both dove into my rough draft when I needed constructive, honest feedback. Justin was there to help with all the ongoing aspects of books and the Internet.

To my friend and editor Sharon Lamson, I have learned a lot from you. Dan Sharp, who is like a brother, not only produced fantastic artwork but also had the patience and talent to reflect my vision on the page. And my thanks go to Heather Mantovani, my good proofer/page designer and team player.

Special thanks to the following people for their outstanding support: Ellen Taylor, Ruth Stricklen, Karen Burd, Lorelee Sheeter, Natali Torres, Doris Stone, Tracy Brogan, Lauren Lopp, Lori Moon, the DeJonges, Shirley Palma, Donna Clark, Sue Spahr, Ellen Anker, Collin Roof, Judy Laux, Mary Bernthal, the Mumma's, Robin Crossman, Natalie Foley and Hayley Cornelisse.

# CONTENTS

# CHAPTER ONE
# THE RED MIST

THE OLD farmhouse was dark and silent, like a tomb. A creaking noise fractured the stillness; Brian woke with a start. "What was that? Anyone there?" he called. He rubbed his eyes and squinted to focus on the illuminated clock: 3:49 a.m.

He threw back the covers and swung his long legs around, letting his bare toes touch the cool wooden floor. Rising to his feet, he caught his balance on the bedpost and staggered down the hallway half awake. "I'd better check in on Cassie," he thought.

Peeking in her room, the sight of her empty bed startled him. Where was she? The bed had been slept in but Cassie was gone.

Bewildered, he began a systematic search of the darkened farmhouse. It had only been three days since she had used the tunnel beneath Blackwater Pond to travel from her world to Brian's.

"She can't be fully adjusted yet," he thought. "The way we do things in this world might not be the norm for her."

As he walked into the living room, the empty rocker was

moving back and forth ever so slightly. No one had sat in it since Grandma had died. "Must be the breeze from the window pushing it," Brian muttered.

Brian finished his search with no luck. Then a troubling thought came to him: *Cassie is at the pond. I can just feel it. I don't know why she would go there, but I am sure that's right where she is.*

Following his instincts he cautiously slipped out the squeaky screen door making sure to close it quietly behind him. The grass in the backyard was shockingly wet and cold against his bare feet. He trotted through the dewy grass toward the outer reaches of their yard. He abruptly stopped where the grass ended and the field began. He knew that crossing that line would throw him into the unknown— once again.

He remembered what happened to him the last time he had snuck out to the pond in the middle of the night. Shivers rippled through him, as he recalled being pulled under by a powerful whirlpool and passing out from lack of air. He had awakened in a tunnel under the pond and followed it to the rubbery membrane. The moment he had stepped through it, his life had changed forever.

He could still vividly see the strange medieval world, controlled by the evil priest Leether, and the carnivorous red clouds. But he reminded himself that he had thrown the crystal into the pond and closed the door forever. "I'm safe in this world. The evil priest and man-eating red cloud can stay in the other one," he said to himself. "The only good thing about that place was Cassie, and she is in my world now."

He felt a chill as the cool night breezes rushed by him. The breeze played off the tall grasses, bowing them down and then pushing them back up again like ocean waves. He stepped into the grassy rip current and was instantly swallowed up. A small sliver of a moon was the only source of light. He took measured steps, as he could scarcely see.

During the past few weeks, the path to the pond had overgrown due to the summer rainstorms. "I doubt too many people go to the pond anymore," he thought. "So many strange stories got dug up when everyone thought Tommy had drowned."

He pushed aside the sharp grass with his hand and continued forward. The cool black muck oozed between his toes. He felt it cling to the bottom of his feet and smelled its earthy scent.

"I should have brought the lantern!" he grumbled. "But I'm not going back for it now. If I just stay on the path it will lead me right up to the water's edge—I hope."

The pond was only a mile or so to the north but, blinded by darkness, it seemed much farther. After an uneasy fifteen-minute walk, he finally pushed through the low willow branches that surrounded the pond. They felt like feathery arms sliding over his shoulders as he walked underneath them. He noticed a dark silhouette sitting against a tree near the shore.

"It's Cassie, sure enough," he thought. "This is very weird. What do I really know about her except that she's from another world? We didn't have much time for chitchat when Leether was chasing us."

As he approached, she calmly turned and smiled at him. It gave him chills. It was as if she were expecting him at that very moment.

"Hi!" she said casually.

"What are you doing?" he asked.

"What do you mean?"

"Night is the time for sleeping."

"I love the night," she said. "It surrounds me like a cool

blanket." She wrapped her arms around herself. "Have you ever stared into the night when it is darker than dark? It looks like thick velvet."

"Velvet? You like the night? Most people are afraid of it."

"Nighttime is mysterious and magical. My cat understood it. Night is the time for the dance of the spirits. It opens your heart and expands your mind. Things that are common and uninteresting in the daylight shine and glisten at night. Come sit and enjoy it with me."

"Okay," he said. Apprehensively he took a seat in the grass next to her. Leaning back against the tree he put an arm around her shoulders. She nuzzled against his cheek and he could feel her soft black hair against his face. She stretched out her slender legs and crossed her bare foot over the top of his.

"It's cool you like the night," Brian said. "What a great way to look at it. Most people think it's creepy…hey, what's with your toes?" He squinted trying to see. "What do you have in-between them? Is that webbing or something?"

"Yes, it is." They both sat in silence for a moment. "I assume by your surprise that you have no toe webbing?" She sat up, frowned, and folded her arms defensively across her chest.

"No webs," he confirmed.

She turned to him and clasped his face in her hands. "Okay, I have toe webs. So what? It doesn't change who I am."

"But it kind of is who you are. I know we're different anyway, because you're a girl, and I am for sure okay with all of the boy-girl differences."

"What we look like is who we are? Do you believe that?" she said. "Don't you care more about who I am on the inside? If I grew horns would you cast me aside like some freakish

4

animal?"

"No, you misunderstood me," he said. To make a point he pressed his open palm over his heart. "Cassie, I care about who you are on the inside. Cross my heart!"

Cassie glanced at him with no amusement. "Nice, but is that where you heart is?"

"Yes," Brian said with a nod.

Cassie smiled weakly. "My heart is on the other side."

"You won't really grow horns will you?" he asked sincerely.

"Stop it!" she yelled.

Brian was puzzled at her response. Not knowing the right thing to say he tried one last time, hoping she would understand. "I know your heart is in the right place. Well, actually, the wrong place—at least as far as where my heart is located. You know what I mean?"

Cassie gave him a cold stare and scowled.

"You must be a good swimmer with those webs." He smiled faintly, still trying to repair the damage of his misspoken words.

"You're making me feel like such a freak. Until now I liked my toes."

The uncomfortable silence became so thick with tension that not another word was said for several minutes. Twilight began to lighten the sky; dawn would arrive soon. The ground was damp with dew and the air, crisp. It felt pure and fresh just to sit and breathe. The freshness of the morning dispelled the tension. "I have lived here all my life and have never seen the pond look so surreal," said Brian, breaking the silence.

"Now, you are beginning to understand the dark," Cassie replied.

Brian observed an eerie red mist intertwined with the white fog that floated inches above the pond. "Probably nothing," he thought. "I never noticed it before, but I have never been at the pond this early. After what I have been through, everything looks scary."

He saw a dark shape emerge from the white haze, on the other side of the pond. It was thin and black. The image slowly grew sharper and jagged, as if cut out of tin.

"Look," he whispered gently into Cassie's ear, as he pointed into the mist.

They both sat completely still, easily blending in with the twilight shadows. Soon the image became completely visible. It was an old woman cradling a bundle of flowers. She wiped one eye with the back of her free hand.

They heard her murmur, "Sarah, I will always love you."

Then they watched as she leaned over and threw the handful of flowers into the water. The flowers floated for a moment, defying the inevitable, and then sank beneath the surface. Standing still as a stone, the woman appeared completely mesmerized.

"Well, I'll be," Brian whispered. "So she's the Flower Witch."

"The who?" asked Cassie?

"My friends and I sometimes find cut flowers in the shallows of the pond. This has gone on for years and years. When we were little, we thought a witch had thrown them in while casting spells. We thought it was the witch's way of asking the pond to take another body or something, but now I know where the flowers actually come from. I wonder who she really is and what she's doing."

"She was crying," Cassie said softly. "I don't think she's a witch. I have never seen a witch cry."

"We don't have real witches in this world, let alone ones that cry, but I will say that this pond seems to have a crying effect on people," said Brian.

Hearing his words, the woman jerked her head up like a frightened deer. She spun and scurried quickly back into the haze.

Brian clamored to his feet, and Cassie raised her hands to fend off his flying elbows as he jumped and ran.

"Wait!" he called out. He raced along the bank waving his hand through the mist. "I want to ask you something!"

By the time he arrived at the other side of the pond, the woman had vanished. Giving up on his chase, he turned his attention to the cool water and the flowers lying on the pond's sandy bottom. He walked into the water to rinse the wet grass and muck from his bare feet.

"Hey, I see something down here in the water."

"Not a good idea, Brian," Cassie said, as she moved toward him. "Haven't you learned your lesson? Don't go out any deeper. Stay out of there!"

"Don't worry. It's okay. I see something in the shallow water." He waded farther in, until the water was up to his waist. Then he reached down, soaking his shirt, and pulled up a spiked black helmet. He held up the helmet by one of the sharp spikes, which ran across the top like a Mohawk. Tipping it back he smiled as the sand and water ran out of it. "Look what I found!"

Cassie entered the pond and waded out to him. She gently slid her arm around his waist. "We should keep it so I can always remember where I came from."

"This is proof that we're not crazy. I am holding onto a knight's helmet from another world! This is the only evidence I have. Even so, who would believe that under the pond lays a doorway to another place?"

"And that doorway is closed. Throwing the crystal into the pond to close the doorway was the right thing to do. I'm glad it's closed. I can take some peace in that, but at the same time it makes me feel like I have lost a little part of myself."

She pushed her cheek against his and looked at their rippled images in the water. "Brian, you have two reflections," she said pointing. "Is that another one of our differences?"

Brian could clearly see Cassie's single reflection. But his reflection was different. A second, faint image overlapped the first.

"This is so strange. You know that in movies vampires have no reflections. But I have two. It must mean something."

"What is a vampire?"

"It's a fictional, blood-sucking, living dead dude."

"Well then, maybe you are not locked in," she said.

"Locked in?"

"Eurus, the wind spirit, said—just before he sent your aura after the crystal—that life energy lives forever and cannot be destroyed. It only changes form. Maybe your life energy is somewhat disconnected from your body. Normally, our auras are locked in. It might be possible that you have become disjointed. Haven't you ever learned about this?"

"I'm guessing your schooling was a little different than mine," said Brian. "So, are you saying that I'm out of alignment?"

"Yes—kind of—I think you are out of sorts or disconnected, whatever word you want to use. Your aura never properly locked back into your body."

"You think?"

"Come on, the sun is coming up. The magic is leaving and so should we." She took his hand and led him toward the shore.

"If my aura is unlocked, how do I get locked in again?" He put the knight's helmet on and followed Cassie onto the grassy bank.

"I don't know. I was just guessing," she said. "I had heard

about it, but I honestly never saw anyone separate from their body until Eurus did it to you."

They walked around the outer bank of the pond and started down the path for home. With each step, the soil under Brian's feet became increasingly soft and unstable. "Hey!" he cried out. His right leg sank knee-deep into gooey black muck. "Agh!" he said, as he fell back to brace himself with both hands. "What the heck! It like sucked me in! I'm stuck! Cassie, grab my arm and pull me out of here!"

Cassie dug her heals into the soft grass behind him to get solid footing. She grasped his arms, leaned back, and pulled hard.

"This is like quicksand or something," said Brian.

"You should be more careful of it."

"We don't have quicksand around here."

"It appears that you do," Cassie said, gasping for breath. She struggled to get a better grip under Brian's arms.

Then Brian felt something deep in the ground coil around his ankle like a snake. "Hey! Something's got a stranglehold on my foot. Pull! Pull!"

He winced in pain as the coil cut into his ankle. "Pull harder!" he screamed, even though Cassie was right next to him.

Cassie strained, grinding her teeth. Her face reddened, and she leaned into it with all she had.

Brian felt his foot going numb. He tried in vain to kick his leg free and move himself toward Cassie. "It's not letting go. It's pulling me down. Let's both tug at the same time! Okay, ready?"

"Ready!" said Cassie. "Let's do it—now!"

They pulled in unison, and, for the first time, he felt it give a little.

"Again!" This time he got most of his leg out. Stinking

black muck covered it.

"Crawl!" she yelled. "You're almost out!" His calf and ankle, still submerged, were tightly entwined by the coiled appendage.

Brian yanked the helmet off his head, gripped the inside webbing, and slammed the spikes into whatever it was that held him. He pounded the spikes several more times into the muck until it released him. As soon as he was free, he rolled out of the mud to safety.

"Wow, you were really stuck! What is going on?" Cassie asked panting.

"That was scary. I might have been dragged underground if it weren't for you."

Cassie knelt beside him and rubbed the mud from his ankle. "Look at these marks." Brian's ankle was noticeably red, and the skin was peeled off in spots. Blood beaded on the surface and then trickled down his ankle.

"Did your foot get hooked on a root or something?"

"It was no root. Whatever had my ankle was alive. Oh man, I thought things were going to be normal when I got back home. It's as if the weird has followed us here. You know what else? I didn't want to say anything, but I noticed a faint red mist by the pond this morning. What if the man-eating cloud never left?"

"I didn't notice any red mist, Brian. We should be safe from Leether and the cloud. Remember, the doorway is closed forever. We both saw Leether disappear into the pond before it closed."

"But I don't understand what just happened. In my world things don't just grab you and pull you into the ground."

"Never?" she asked.

"Well, not unless you're caught by a boa constrictor in an African jungle or something."

"Oh, so things like this can happen in your world. I don't know how normal it is for you, but at moments like this my father would have said: 'This is more likely the beginning of something than the end of it.'"

Brian rubbed his ankle. "Mom wanted us to walk over to the farmers market for her today. I hope I can make it on this beat-up ankle."

"If you can't walk I'll help you," Cassie said with a smile.

"You are one tough cookie," Brian said.

"I think you probably have some tough cookies, too— whatever that is supposed to mean." She laughed. "What would a tough cookie look like? I bet it would be so hard that you couldn't bite into it."

Brian stood and put some weight on his tender ankle. "I think it's going to be okay." He took a few steps. "Yeah, I just need to clean it up and get a bandage from Mom."

· · ·

They arrived back home just as the morning shadows began stretching toward them. Brian opened the back screen door for Cassie without a word. The door squeaked loudly, giving them away. To make matters worse, the door slipped from Brian's muddy finger tips and slammed shut with a bang.

His mom shuffled toward the door in her pink bathrobe just as Brian and Cassie walked into the kitchen. "Brian, you have got to fix that squeaky door!"

Then she took a good look at them and raised an eyebrow. "Hey, where have you two been? Is that helmet what I think it is? You're tracking mud everywhere! Stop right there! Brian, are you bleeding?"

Brian took a deep breath and replied, "At the pond; yes it

is; I'll stop tracking; and yes I am."

Cassie giggled, "You answered all of her questions."

"Years of practice," he mumbled out of the corner of his mouth.

Mom picked up a damp cloth from the kitchen sink, lifted his foot, and began to clean the blood and mud from his ankle before he could say another word. "What happened here? Your ankle is all scraped up. Did you trip over something?"

"Hey, Mom, guess who I saw?" he said, attempting to change the subject. "The Flower Witch." He turned on the faucet and rinsed the helmet in the sink, while bouncing on one foot. "There was this scary-looking old lady and…"

"Did she hurt your ankle?"

"Nah, she ran off."

Mom frowned. "What does seeing the Flower Witch have to do with your ankle?"

"Nothing."

"I have no chance of making any sense of this, do I?"

Cassie shook her head. "No, you have no chance."

# CHAPTER TWO
# THE FRIGHTENING

AFTER AN early-morning breakfast, Brian felt comfortable enough to join Tommy and Cassie as they headed for the farmers market. The sun rose above the fields as they walked beneath a shady oak and across their front yard toward the dry gravel road. An easy smile spread across Tommy's freckled face, as his pin-straight blond hair blew back in the morning breeze.

Cassie stepped up her stride to walk between the two of them. "Is your ankle going to be okay?" Cassie asked Brian, as they started down the road.

"Doesn't hurt to walk on it. Mom overkilled it with the bandaging and made it too tight, but I guess it's alright."

Cassie shielded her eyes with her hand. "The sun is so bright it actually hurts to look at it," she said. "I can feel its warmth. It's like sitting too close to a campfire! If we kept walking, I bet eventually we would walk right into it."

"Yeah, it's different from the sun in your world, isn't it? You're going to have a ton of new things to get used to."

"What is this place?" she asked in amazement, throwing up her hands as a car drove by, kicking up dust.

"This is 59 Matthew Street."

"That's the name of this world?"

"Oh, no—it's called Earth."

"What does Earth mean?"

"It's earth—you know—dirt. You could pick up a handful of earth."

"Your world is named after dirt?"

"Well, what's the name of your world?" he asked.

"Aphelion Chiasm. Aphelion means, 'farthest from the light,' and Chiasm means, 'the intersection of two different paths.'"

"Weird name."

"At least it's not named after dirt," she said.

"Good point."

"I've been thinking about how the membrane actually works," said Tommy, changing the subject.

"I think we all have," said Brian. "That membrane must be a portal between the two worlds."

Tommy shrugged. "Our crazy friend Ebil would have an answer. You would probably have to decode his rhyme to figure it out though."

"With the membrane closed, we will never see him again," said Brian.

The trio continued down the dusty road toward the market several miles away. The air was thick with pollen and buzzing beetles. The bugs were always loudest when a hot steamy day was ahead.

Brian kept a comfortable stride despite his injured ankle. He looked forward to the fresh new day ahead of them. Everything seemed so perfect.

They walked past a big green cornfield that stretched all the way back to the train tracks. The farmhouse and barn in the distance looked like small red and white dots.

Cassie peered between the narrow, endless, overgrown rows of corn. "They're all in a perfect line, one after the other. This is a nice, orderly world, isn't it?"

"Basically," said Brian. "But it all depends on where you are." Then he stopped at the beginning of one of the rows. "Wait! Did you see that?"

Cassie squinted toward the place where Brian was pointing. "What?"

"I thought I saw something moving through the corn."

"Are you getting skittish? Don't worry; you have no deadly red clouds here, no evil beasts, no Leether trying to kill us. You should enjoy what you do have: interesting machines, a big yellow sun, and tall orderly plants."

Brian put a brotherly arm on Tommy's shoulder. "To think we have Joey to thank for everything. If he hadn't dared you to touch the bottom of the pond, none of this would have happened. I guess you never know what small event is going to set off a chain reaction."

"That Joey kid always bugs me," said Tommy. "I'd love to wipe that stupid grin off his freckly face. I'll dunk him next time we're at the pond."

"But what if it's winter?" asked Cassie.

"Then I'll wash his face in the snow."

"The desert?" Brian smiled.

"If we're in a desert, I'll make him eat sand."

Brian smiled broadly. "On the moon?"

"I would smash his face in a mound of moldy cheese," Tommy said with a laugh.

Suddenly, from the corner of his eye, Brian caught a glimpse of something yellow. He reacted by ducking and covering his head with his arms. A corncob nicked his ear and landed next to him on the road. Several cornstalks moved.

"Who's out there?" Tommy yelled.

There was faint laughter.

"Come out of there!" Brian demanded.

Two more corncobs sailed out of the field, as if launched from a cannon. "I see where you are this time," Brian said.

Tommy dodged one, but in doing so stepped into the path of another. It glanced off his shoulder. "Ouch!"

Brian zeroed in on the location of the last corncob launching, veered from the road, and hurdled over a splintered wooden fence. "Who's the idiot?" he yelled.

Once he entered the field, he was dwarfed by the height of the corn. Looking down, Brian made out tennis shoe prints in the dusty brown soil, cutting between the cornstalks. He pushed aside the stalks and followed the footprints over a few more rows. He glanced up in time to see someone in a yellow shirt running in the opposite direction. As he peered down the length of a long row of corn, he observed the person bobbing and weaving between the rows. The wild red hair tossing in the wind identified the guilty.

"Joey, the idiot," he muttered. "Chasing you is a waste of time." Frustrated, Brian jumped the fence and returned to the road, slightly winded.

"Who was it?" Tommy asked, as Brian limped alongside of them.

"Take a guess. It was that little jerk Joey. What's wrong with that kid? He must have been shadowing us and overheard you cutting him down. I have never met anyone who enjoyed being a pain in the butt more than he does. I think he's headed for the railroad tracks on the backside of the cornfield. He can run down the tracks and then get off to hide anywhere he likes. It could take the rest of the day to track him down, and he isn't worth the effort."

"He has a bad case of jerk face," said Tommy.

"By the way, Tom, where were you?"

"What?"

"I thought you would be right behind me. What if there had been trouble? You are my wing-man," he said.

Tommy made a face. "Oh, sorry. I guess I thought you had it handled."

"I'm just a little insulted," said Cassie, her hands on her hips.

"Huh?" said Brian.

"You should be yelling at me, too! I am part of your team, right? I expect to be treated equally."

"I was just glad you were safe on the road."

"If we are to have a bond then it must be a bond of equal risk. I risk for you and you risk for me. You are my wings and I am yours."

"Got it," said Brian. He scolded her with one raised finger. "You should have gone in with me."

Cassie smiled. "That's right. I should have! Now who is this Joey?"

Tommy piped up, "He is the village jerk. He always hassles me. Like Brian said, he was the one who dared me to touch the bottom of the pond."

"When we thought you had drowned, he just sat there on the raft," said Brian. "He never said he was sorry. He looked like he couldn't care less."

Tommy rolled his eyes. "He's a psycho."

"Psychopath?" Brian said. "That might be overstating it a little. The kid is a jerk for sure, but I don't know about a psycho."

"Remember those dead rabbits Dave found tied to the railroad tracks? He figured that someone had tied them up and had the train run over them for fun. Who does that?"

"Joey, the psychopath?" Brian said.

Brian's mouth curled into a small grin. "Okay, you've

analyzed this kid all the way from jerk-face right up to serial-killer-apprentice in about two seconds. He's not that bad. He probably just needs to outgrow the jerkiness."

"Let's just forget this Joey creature and enjoy the rest of our walk," Cassie suggested.

They turned down a two-track road toward a large red barn. Brian pulled Cassie to the side just as a rusty blue pickup truck with a mismatching brown fenders barreled by. It had baskets of corn bouncing in the back.

Along the road was a grassy open area with more pickup trucks backed up to colorful makeshift canopies and overhangs. Each farmer had set up a booth and staked claim to his or her very own special space. The workers carefully displayed their produce atop folding tables. The farmers market was abuzz with activity.

"How does this work?" asked Cassie.

"It's no big deal," Brian answered. "Most people just come here to swap stories and buy stuff. We usually start at one end and work our way up and down each row. Let me know if you see something that interests you."

Crowds of people moved around the tables. Many customers had wisely shown up early and parked behind the barn. They clearly wanted to get the first pick of the fresh fruits, vegetables, and breads.

Brian, Tommy, and Cassie started at the end of the first row of tables. Taking his time, Brian closely examined the fresh baked bread and the baskets full of shiny red tomatoes. Cassie followed Brian while Tommy wandered off on his own.

Brian noticed an old woman staring at Cassie from across the aisle and down several tables. The woman was placing red canning jars next to bundles of cut flowers. She continued to put the jars in neat rows on the table—all the while fixing her gaze on Cassie.

"What's with that lady?" Brian said. "She won't stop staring."

"Where?" asked Cassie.

"Over there," Brian said, pointing past a small pyramid of glistening red apples. Brian tried to focus through the maze of activity. He could just make out the old woman whose face and steel gray hair were hit hard by the morning sun. Her neatly pressed dress was covered with muted shades of blue flowers. She shielded her eyes with one hand, but otherwise stood as if frozen by Cassie's image.

"That woman, she…interests me," said Cassie.

Brian bent close to Cassie's ear. "I am almost positive she's the same one we saw at the pond this morning."

"I wonder what's wrong with her." Cassie said. "Uh-oh, she's moving. Oh boy, here she comes."

The woman moved toward them, all the while maintaining her stare. As she went around a fruit-laden table, she inadvertently stumbled over a full basket of tomatoes. The tomatoes broke free and rolled across the ground. The woman caught her balance with one hand on a folding chair and continued toward them, paying no attention to the runaway fruit. Then she cut between several people, disrupting their conversation, and dodged a woman walking toward her. Intent on Cassie, the woman tripped a little over a sleeping cocker spaniel, and then came straight toward them.

Despite the old woman's small stature and obvious inability to inflict any meaningful harm, Brian felt guarded.

Finally, the woman stopped directly in front of Cassie. She reached out slowly and lightly touched Cassie's arm with her trembling hand. "What's your name, dear?" the woman asked softly.

She stared at Cassie with such intensity that Brian

wondered if the woman had even noticed he was there.

"Cassie—my name is Cassie."

"You have a strong resemblance to someone who was very special to me—your eyes, your nose, and even the shape of your face." The woman reached up with a shaking hand. She slipped her fingers into Cassie's hair, moving some of the strands away from her left ear. Gently, she rubbed the bottom of Cassie's earlobe.

Cassie didn't move. "What are you doing?" she asked. "Are you the flower witch?"

"Witch?" The old woman smiled. "No, I'm feeling for the family bump. I know this must seem terribly odd to you, but I just had to check. Most everyone in my ancestry has this little telltale bump right here on the bottom of the ear," she said holding Cassie's earlobe. "My cousin Johnny doesn't have the bump, but we aren't really sure if he's related. You see, his Mama left town and..."

"I assure you, we can't be related," Cassie said, smiling. She politely and gently took the old shaky hand from her ear.

"You have a most unusual accent. Where are you from, dear?"

"Aphelion Chiasm," said Cassie.

"Can't say I have ever heard of it. Is it closeby?"

"Yes and no."

"Yes and no? Well, my, that was an unusual answer, wasn't it?" The woman cocked her head to one side. "What is your mother's name?"

"Trust me, she can't be related to you," Brian interrupted. "Compare toes if you don't believe me," he said with a grin.

Cassie frowned at the comment.

"Toes?" asked the puzzled old woman.

Just then Brian saw Tommy running toward them, zigzagging between people in the crowded market. He bounded up to them, the back of his head caked with tomato pulp. "Joey's trying to nail me! Hide me, quick!"

Whop! Brian felt the stinging impact of a tomato slap hard against his face. He quickly dug the pulp from his eye. Glancing up, he saw Joey Hasselback racing toward them, throwing tomatoes with great exuberance. People scrambled to get out of the way.

"Oh my!" said the old woman. "What is this, now?"

"What are you hiding for, Tom?" Brian yelled, as he ducked an incoming tomato. "Get up! Get ready!"

Tommy glanced up at Brian, from his defensive crouching position.

Brian motioned for him to stand, which Tommy did.

Joey let the last tomato fly, and then like a charging bull, stampeded toward them. Just before impact, he stretched out his arms in front of him and locked his elbows. Using his arms as battering rams, he hit Tommy hard with both hands at full speed.

Tommy took the shot to his chest and was knocked off balance. His backward momentum sent him reeling into the helpless old woman. Being no match for this kind of brute force, she was thrown to the ground. Her head smacked the hard dirt. She lay there motionless.

"You just crossed the line," Brian snarled, as he gritted his teeth. "That does it." He jumped over his fallen brother and sprinted after Joey, who raced off through the crowd. Bystander's yelled things like, "Hey!" and "Slow down!" But the battle was on, and Brian didn't want anything to stop it. He knew something big was about to happen, like shifting snow moments before an avalanche.

As Brian dashed through the crowd, he heard Tommy frantically apologizing to the old woman. "Oh ma'am, I am so sorry!"

Glancing back, Brian saw Tommy jump up and join him in the chase.

Joey dodged and weaved his way through the crowd, bouncing off startled people. Once clear of the crowd, he headed for the safety of an old barn, with Brian and Tommy in hot pursuit.

"It's time to even the score," Brian growled under his breath. He knew that all the abuse Joey had dealt Tommy over the years was going to be paid back in full at any moment.

Joey cleared the threshold of the barn door and slammed it shut as hard as he could.

The door struck Brian's body solidly, jolting his full sprint to a dead stop in an instant. His body remained frozen on impact, but his momentum separated his aura from his body. It left his body and passed through the closed barn door. Brian was once again a silvery ghost.

Joey leaned against the door panting and laughing. He tugged on a rope, which dropped a small plank across the door and locked it. In his excitement he didn't see Brian's aura floating just a few feet above his head. The only noise had been a thud, as Brian's body connected with the door.

"Oh my gosh," Brian thought. "I don't know what just happened to me but I've got to take advantage of this. I hope I can make a convincing ghost." He smiled when he realized how strange his life had become. "I would have never guessed that being a convincing ghost would be a goal of mine."

Seemingly satisfied that Brian was probably knocked out on the other side of the door, Joey barely noticed the flicker of light overhead. Then he glanced up and saw Brian, the floating specter.

"AAAAAHHHH!" screamed Joey in a rather girly, high-pitched squeal. He panicked and frantically tried to dislodge the locking board. But it was wedged in tight. Joey pushed hard and banged on it with the palms of his hands.

"Oooooo!" Brian said in a breathy voice, doing his best to sound scary. "Joey, don't go. Come join me in the land of the dead, you red-haired freckle-faced freak. You must spend eternity with me in a filthy, rotten, smelly, disgusting, stench pit of icy death and decay. Come! You must join me, you, obnoxious jerk! Ah-ha-ha-ha!"

Joey's face paled, his eyes popped open wide, and his breaths came in short bursts. The board Joey was fumbling with finally popped up. He was able to compose himself enough to yank the door open, but as he attempted to dash to freedom he stepped right into Tommy.

Brian watched Tommy angrily snatch a large handful of Joey's shirt and twist it until it became taut. Tommy glared into Joey's crazed eyes, reached back, and doubled his fist tightly. Then he thrust his entire body into the punch and caught Joey squarely under the chin with an uppercut. Joey's head snapped back, and he went down flat on his back. Tommy stood over him while Joey lay in shock, staring up at him. "Go on, run, you jerky, creep butt!" Tommy yelled.

"Ahhhhh!" Joey screamed, as he scratched and stumbled to his feet. Then he took off like a wounded dog. In a flash he had disappeared into the cornfield and was gone.

Tommy knelt over Brian's body, which was still in a frozen state lying on the ground. He shook his shoulders. "Brian! Get back in, will ya? You're creeping me out!"

Brian's aura floated over his body and fell inside. He slowly opened his eyes and smiled. "Nice punch, Tom!"

"It was awesome!" Tommy grinned. "I cleaned his clock, didn't I?"

"Yeah, you really clocked him. The clock is clean."

"I knocked him into the next time zone."

"Hey, did you see me? I completely separated from my

body! I guess my aura isn't locked in anymore."

"Yeah, I saw. It was really amazing. Can you do it anytime you want?"

"I have no idea. I think the barn door dislodged my aura or something. Hey, did you see Joey's face? That was so great. I loved it. And, Tom, that punch—wow! It was awesome."

"I must admit it felt really good," said Tommy. "I feel like Iron Mike Tyson."

"I got a good scare into him, and then it was just great when he walked right into you," said Brian.

"Yeah, I could hear you on the other side of the door. You got pretty creepy with that land of the dead stuff. It was even starting to freak me out."

"I was going for effect. What about you and that bit about jerky, creep, butt? Ha-ha! That was the best you could come up with?"

They both laughed out loud.

Brian slowly got to his feet and put his hand on Tommy's arm. "We'd better get back to the market."

"I don't think Joey will ever forget this day," Tommy said, as he laughed.

"I think we made a memory."

Tommy snickered. "Or at least a nightmare." Then in a more serious tone, he added, "Hey, did you see the old woman go down when I got pushed? I hope she's okay."

"I know! It happened so fast. I think Cassie is probably still with her."

# CHAPTER THREE
# THE FLOWER WITCH

WHEN BRIAN and Tommy got back to Cassie, she was gently cradling the unconscious woman's head. Blood trickled from the wound on her temple. Its dark red color stood in stark contrast to her pale white skin. A helpful farm girl handed Cassie a damp towel, which she gently but firmly pressed over the cut.

The old woman's wrinkled eyelids fluttered and slowly opened. She gazed into Cassie's eyes. "Sarah," the woman said weakly. "You mustn't leave your doll collection lying about. I always keep tripping over them."

Cassie shook her head. "I'm so sorry. I am not your Sarah."

Brian asked, "Sarah who?" He squatted next to the woman, hoping he could more easily hear her breathy voice.

"She must think I'm someone named Sarah," said Cassie.

The woman shook her head a bit and jarred herself back into full consciousness. "No, you're right. You are not my Sarah," said the old woman, speaking more clearly. "They never found her. She went into that pond, and it never gave her back."

The woman began to sob with such pain; it was as if

25

she had lost her Sarah only moments earlier. "She was only thirteen. She was my very special girl."

Cassie gave the woman a hug for a lingering moment and then helped her sit upright. Cassie maintained firm pressure on the woman's wound.

With glossy eyes, now only inches from Cassie's face, the woman peered at her and said, "You look just like my Sarah. That's why I came up to you. I'm sorry. I know it must seem very odd of me, but I see her in you. Even the way you just tilted your head."

"So sorry," Cassie said. "I wish I could be your Sarah, but I'm not." She gave the woman a warm embrace.

"Your voice, it is—unmistakable."

When Cassie pulled away, her sapphire necklace swung away from her throat and dangled in front of the woman's eyes.

"That necklace! Where did you get it?" The old woman caught it in her trembling hand.

"It was my mother's."

The old woman's eyes widened. "This is the same stone that I had cut for Sarah on her thirteenth birthday, and it was around her neck when she went into the pond some thirty years ago. It's a blue sapphire—her birthstone."

"Who are you?" Cassie asked.

"My name is Rae—short for Raven. Did you find the necklace in the pond?"

"No," Cassie answered. "Like I told you, it was given to me by my mother."

"Did your mother find it in the pond?"

"No."

"What was your mother's name?"

Cassie paused, almost afraid to answer. "Sarah."

"Where is your mother?" The old woman's gray eyes

welled with emotion. Tears pooled in her eyes and rolled down her cheeks.

"I never met her. She died in childbirth, and as far as the necklace goes, I was told that she wanted me to have it."

"But how can that be?"

"It can't be. My mom must be a different Sarah, and this must be a different necklace."

The woman turned the necklace over and held it closely in her hand. Squinting, she tilted it slightly, and when it caught the morning light just right she was able to read the worn inscription on the back. "'To Sarah. Love eternally.' This is definitely my Sarah's necklace. Look right here, I had it engraved myself. Tell me how this is possible."

"If my mother was also your daughter then there are many things to unravel."

She took notice of all the busy people who, despite their preoccupied appearances, were probably eavesdropping. She glanced at Brian, and then said to Rae, "You and I need some time to talk alone, so we can sort this out."

A middle-aged woman, who had obviously been listening, stepped into view. "I'll work the table for you, Rae. Don't worry about a thing. I'll pick up your jars of sauce and flowers and wrap things up for you when the market closes. Would you kids mind seeing her home? And please put some ice on her head."

Brian nodded. "Don't worry, we will get her home."

To Tommy he said, "Can you head back to the farm and tell Mom we are going to be awhile?"

"Okay, I'll go," said Tommy, looking a little disappointed that he would be missing the action.

"Luckily, I only live a mile from here as the crow flies," Rae said, and she pointed up the hill to a winding dirt road. The homes up there were almost obscured by trees. Parts of the porches and rooftops peaked out here and there from the top of the wooded rise.

Cassie helped Rae to her feet. The woman steadied herself by holding onto Cassie's arm. They slowly made their way up the dirt road and turned left at the fork. Before long they came to Rae's small but sprawling rural neighborhood. Rae was mostly silent during the slow walk, but she kept glancing at Cassie and smiling now and again.

"Do I have that family earlobe bump?" asked Cassie.

"Yes, you do."

Cassie felt her own ear and nodded. "Guess so."

They had started up the steep, paved street that led to Rae's house, when the morning breeze kicked up without warning. It caused a small whirlwind to spin around them. "Brrrrian," it hissed. "Eeeeevil works against ussssssss."

"I hear those voices again," said Rae.

"It's okay—so do we," said Brian.

Rae put her hand on his face. "You do? Oh my, that makes me feel so much better. I have heard voices off and on for the last thirty years and just figured I was going bats. It kept asking me to come to the pond. I have done my best to ignore it. Normally, I hum a tune or clear my throat a few times, and then it always goes away."

"Evil works against us?" Brian thought. "Is that Eurus trying to warn me about this old lady? My instincts tell me she's okay."

Brian felt an eerie sensation that someone was watching him. He jerked around, hoping to catch a glimpse of whoever was spying on them, but no one was there.

Near the top of the hill sat an older cottage-style, two-story home with stained glass windows. The front yard was so overgrown with vibrant flowers and plants that the lawn was hidden. A classic white-picket fence bordered the property.

They stepped onto the curb, and Rae pointed toward the front walk. "This is the place."

The wind whistled by and blasted against the sides of the house, kicking up leaves and branches. "Brrrrian, all may not be is as it seems. I am losing controoool."

"Oh my!" said Rae. "It's that voice again, and it is obviously talking to you, Brian. Who are you people?"

"Flesh and blood," said Cassie. "Like you."

Out of habit, Cassie scanned the sky. She noticed the faint glimmer of a small, misty cloud with an orange-red tint. "We've got to get inside," she said, pushing Brian ahead. "We are exposed out here in the open!"

"Exposed to what?" Brian asked. Then, following Cassie's gaze, he saw the red cloud lurking overhead. "But, how can that be? There aren't any red clouds in this world!"

They each put an arm around Rae's waist and hustled her up the walk toward the front door.

"W-what is going on?" Rae stammered, as she ran with her feet barely touching the ground.

"It's Leether the cloud priest!" yelled Cassie. "One of his clouds has stuck around in this world."

Rae froze. "What?"

"Quick! Unlock the door!" cried Cassie.

Rae fumbled nervously for a key in her baggy dress pocket.

Cassie locked eyes with Brian. "A piece of the cloud must have been left behind. What if Leether is controlling it from Aphelion Chiasm? He could be watching us right now!"

"Who are you people?" Rae asked again. With a glance that showed her bewilderment, she found the correct key. However, her hand shook so hard, she kept missing the keyhole.

Brian guided her hand, and together they pushed the key

solidly into the slot. With the door unlocked, they pushed through the door to safety, spilling into a small living room. Cassie closed and locked the door behind them.

"Leether is obsessed," Cassie said to Brian. "He cannot rest until justice is done for Nimbus. We are in danger as long as any part of the cloud is on this side of the membrane and knows where we are. Close all the windows."

Rae stood in the living room watching Brian and Cassie scurry past her, going from room to room. "You people are so strange, so strange indeed. What to do? I could make tea."

Brian and Cassie panted as they entered the kitchen. Rae had already taken out several of her fine teacups and was placing them around her small circular kitchen table.

"Sit!" she ordered, pointing at the chairs like a military general.

"First, I need to put some ice on your head," said Cassie. "I promised the nice woman at the market."

"My old head can wait. Please sit."

The teakettle began to whistle as Cassie and Brian took their seats. Rae poured the steaming water into their cups and dropped in tea bags.

Cassie took a sip of the tea and put her nose right up to the cup. She took a deep whiff and said, "Mmm."

Rae pulled up a chair, sat down next to her, and leaned close. "I find myself both fascinated and frightened by you, my dear."

"I could say the same about you," said Cassie.

"Why don't you start talking about who you are, where you're from, and end with that little red cloud?"

"I came up through the pond three days ago," Cassie said.

"You came up through the pond?" questioned Rae. "I don't understand what you mean. Please be absolutely clear."

Cassie looked at Brian. "Well okay," she said, "Just realize that what I'm about to say will probably sound very strange to you. So, please just roll with it."

Rae leaned back and rubbed her head. She clasped her hands tightly together, as if to prepare for what was to follow.

Cassie continued, "Understand, I am only putting some of this together at this moment. Two things I know for certain: First, there is a tunnel beneath the pond, and it leads to a membrane, which is a kind of one-way portal into my world." Then with watery eyes, she continued, "Second, you are my grandmother. Your Sarah didn't drown in the pond. She went through the membrane, lived on, and married King Bara—my father—in another world. Then she gave birth to me."

Rae broke into tears. They both stood, and she held Cassie tightly to her. "I want to believe you. I know in my heart you are her daughter. It is as plain as the freckles on your face. But I can't pretend to understand any of this," she said, her tears dripping past her wrinkled smile. Rae stood back to look at Cassie's face. "And who is this Leether character who follows you with the red cloud?"

"Well, before I was born, Leether claimed to have the ability to talk to the man-eating red clouds called Nimbus. He made a fire with blue-leaf oil to draw it in like a cat to catnip. As he knelt in the Valley of Tears, a cloud descended but did not harm him. Instead of consuming Leether, the cloud seeped into his every pore—every opening. It melted into him, and Leether became the cloud's host. They shared each other's mind.

"It was after this that he was appointed as the Nimbus priest. He said the clouds would protect us from evil if we would bow down and give sacrifice to them. Whenever the cloud became angry it would drip down and take someone. Leether said that the cloud was protecting us from nonbelievers—like plucking a weed from the flowerbed.

"I was told that my mother fought against Leether's crazy ideals but she died during my birth. Her death threw my father into a shattered mental state. This is when Leether was able to turn him. Leether convinced him that I was a demon seed who caused the death of his Sarah.

"Ever since I was born, Leether has had absolute control over my father's kingdom. Sacrifices to the cloud are given regularly. No one dares to question it. To challenge Leether is to become the cloud's next meal."

Cassie took a deep breath and continued. "Tommy and Brian accidentally went through the membrane into my world. After plenty of trouble they managed to bring me back here with them, but Leether and his cloud followed. Until now we thought we had chased Leether and the cloud back to Aphelion Chiasm for good, but apparently part of the red cloud got left behind somehow. Now the cloud stalks us to make sure justice is done—to ensure we're sacrificed. Once it is decreed that a person is to be sacrificed to the cloud, there is no going back."

Rae looked perplexed.

"None of this makes sense to you, does it?" said Brian.

Rae shook her head. "I fear you are both a bit touched, but I did hear the voice, too, and that red cloud is different from anything I have ever seen in all my years. I truly understand less now than when you started talking. I want to believe you, but I live in a rational world where everything can be explained. Obviously, you two do not. But I do see my daughter in you, Cassie, and I guess that is good enough for me."

She reached back and took a picture from the dinette. "This was your mother at thirteen," she said, holding the framed photo in front of Cassie.

Tears welled in Cassie's eyes. "She does look like me!"

"She always loved the smell of fresh cut flowers. I throw them into the pond because that is as close as I can get to laying them on her grave."

"You're the flower witch," said Brian.

The woman nodded and frowned slightly. Brian cleared his throat. "I don't mean you are a witch. I just meant you're the one we thought was a witch, which is true except for the witch part."

"That was clear," Cassie said with a sarcastic smile.

• • •

The compelling conversations went on late into the evening. Cassie learned her mother had loved gymnastics and horseback riding. Despite her feminine looks, she was a rough-and-tumble girl. She would climb the tree next to the house and jump barefoot onto the roof to get into her second floor bedroom, when the front door would have been easier.

Brian and Cassie stayed the entire day. They ate lunch there and then helped Rae fix dinner: Rae cooked a roast; Cassie mashed the potatoes; Brian set the table. Cassie could not get herself to leave, and Rae didn't want her to. From time to time Brian peeked out the window. The cloud had not moved. It was high in the sky hanging over the house like a vulture waiting for them to make a move.

"What are we going to do?" Cassie asked at dinner. "The cloud is still there. Leether will stalk us forever."

Brian agreed. "He never seemed like the kind of guy to quit easily."

"Leether is tireless—I heard he never even sleeps. Think of the advantage of never needing to rest. He can plan and make moves until he catches us off guard. He can lie in wait for the first opportunity."

"I just don't have the answer to this one," said Brian. "What do we do?"

"Maybe this will help. I have a little magic," said Rae, pulling a small pendulum attached to a string out of her dress pocket. She pinched the top of the string, held it aloft, and watched as the pendulum spun and sparkled. "It's not really magic, but it is the best I can do. I will show you. Brian, take it in your hand and hold the string steady above the table. If you ask it a question it will answer."

"Does it talk?"

"No," Rae said with a smile. "The power is really inside you."

"How accurate is it?"

"Well, let's see. I've tried to keep track. Out of thirteen times, it was correct seven of them, so I would say better than fifty percent."

"Or is it actually right fifty percent of the time, so the next one would be wrong to make it seven for fourteen?"

"Right," Cassie interjected. "If you know it will be wrong next, we could just do the opposite."

Rae rubbed her head. "Oh my! You two have a way of confusing everything. Why is it I feel that the longer I know you, the more confounded I will get?"

"Okay," said Brian. "Why not try it anyway? Here is question one: Should we attempt to go back home, with the red cloud stalking us?"

The pendulum moved counterclockwise.

"Okay, that was a no. Probably good advice," Brian said.

Cassie nodded in agreement.

Brian turned to Rae and asked, "But can this thing tell me how this is all going to end? Why is the wind telling me to beware? How do we kill the cloud?"

"Oh, no—one question at a time!" said Rae, as she clasped her face. "And make sure you only ask good spirits, like angels."

The pendulum suddenly started spinning on the end of the string, like a top. The string snapped at the base and the pendulum bounced onto the table. Whirling wildly it jumped and clanged from plates to cups, and finally landed in Cassie's lap.

"Wow!" said Brian, with a laugh. "What does that mean?"

"It means…" Rae began. "I don't know."

"That's what it means—'I don't know'?"

"Well, I've never seen that happen before. You are obviously not like the rest of us—either of you." She pointed her bent finger at them. "The truth is that good or bad—victory or failure—will always depend on the moves you make, and it is your move."

"So you're saying that it's us against Leether. It's my move—like in chess or checkers."

"Well, yes, I suppose so, if it is that Leether character who competes with you."

"Leether against us in a deadly game of strategy—well, that takes care of that," Brian said. "If it's my move then I say we stay put. We spend the night. It's getting dark and too hard to see, and it's not safe for us to leave with the cloud hovering out there. At least in the morning we can see it in the sky."

"Spend the night. Yes, I would like that," said Rae.

"Or perhaps the cloud cannot see us as well in the night," said Cassie. "But if you want to stay, then I say we stay."

Brian called home and did his best to explain the situation. He urged his mother and brother to stay inside until he could figure out a way to elude the cloud. "It's like

Leether has this thing on remote control and it's waiting in the shadows for us."

Despite the gloom outside, they still had a pleasant evening with Rae. Cassie and Rae sat on the carpet, their backs against the sofa, and looked at old photo albums. When it got late, Rae made up the sofa for Cassie. Brian noted that she seemed to take a special pleasure in just being involved in Cassie's life. After all, Cassie had been denied a mother, and Rae a daughter.

Rae gave them each a cup of hot chocolate before they all retired for the evening. Brian volunteered to sleep on the floor, next to the sofa.

Relaxed for the first time in weeks, Brian had no trouble falling asleep. His conscious mind let go and he lay still as a stone.

For as long as he could remember, Brian tended to have vivid, lifelike dreams. As a small child, his imagination was overpowering, and he would wake wracked with fear at the frightful contrivances of his own making. Now that he was older these kinds of nightmares came less frequently, but still, at times, his subconscious visions felt like reality.

Now, in the deep realms of sleep, he began to experience a lucid dream. He was again an aura hovering for a moment over his own body lying on the rug and Cassie curled up on the sofa. He floated through the ceiling into the attic and then into the night sky. He was weightless as he flew over the speckled lights of the small farm town.

The red cloud came at him from above. He sailed through it without fear. Untouched, he sped off while the cloud pursued.

He approached his family's inconspicuous little farm and circled like a bird of prey. Then he dove toward the house and slid though the walls like a hot knife through butter. As he glided through the outer wall and into the living room, he abruptly bumped a table lamp and sent it crashing onto the hardwood floor. "Oh yeah," he thought. "Eurus said I can touch but can't be touched."

"Brian?" said a familiar voice. A ghostly form sat in the rocker, tipping it slowly back and forth.

"Grandma?"

Apprehensively, he floated to the front of the chair. It was Grandma—looking much stronger and younger. She drifted up from the chair and turned toward him as they both hovered only inches from the tall ceiling. "I have been with you," she said.

"I know. I can feel it, but I have missed you anyway, Gram."

"I didn't follow the light because I knew you would need me here. Worlds are changing. The wind is fading. The great evil grows." She reached out to touch him and her hand passed through his aura. "Things are growing darker."

Suddenly the serene moment was shattered by a piercing scream. "Ieeee!" Brian heard his mother scream. She stood in the room looking up at them, her open mouth frozen in terror.

Brian, shocked into consciousness, woke with a start. He sat up wide-eyed. "Wow! Don't I have normal dreams anymore?" He wiped the beaded sweat from his forehead with his sleeve.

Cassie awoke. "Who are you talking to?"

"Well, myself, I guess. I'm beginning to realize things will never ever be the same."

"Might as well face it, fate has taken us down a different path and there is no going back," said Cassie.

"I just had a dream that I was a floating aura again. I went home and was talking to my dead grandma."

"Whoa, that's so creepy! Were you scared?"

"Oh, no—it wasn't creepy at all because I know she loves me. I could never be afraid of her. She said she has been watching over us. She wanted to warn me."

"What did she say?"

"The wind is fading and things are worse than they appear. Maybe Eurus, our voice in the wind, is in trouble. I feel like we should get back home to make sure Mom and Tommy are okay. I don't care what time it is."

"Okay, I'm with you. I would rather take on the cloud at night anyway."

"Yeah, nighttime is your time, isn't it? Maybe we're making too big a deal out of such a little cloud. How much harm could it do?"

"Maybe it's not even out there anymore."

He wrote a note to Rae, thanking her for her hospitality and explaining why they left. Then he left it on the kitchen table next to her broken pendulum.

As they left, Cassie said, "It was a defining moment in my life to meet her." She held her clenched fist to her heart. "I have a grandma!"

"Don't worry. You'll see her again. We can come back here anytime you want."

# CHAPTER FOUR
# ON DEATH'S DOOR

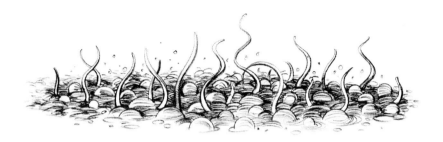

THEY STEPPED into Rae's empty one-stall garage. Brian flicked on the light and scanned the walls looking for anything they could use as a weapon. "Take this," he said, handing some trimming sheers to Cassie. Then he grabbed an old coal shovel off a hook. "We can return these next time we come over."

"What is this for?" asked Cassie, holding up the sheers.

"To protect ourselves."

"Okay, I don't know how we would protect ourselves with these, but I like it anyway. It gives us an excuse to come back."

Cassie opened the side door to the garage and peeked out. All was dark and peaceful. By all accounts it was a pleasant summer night. She looked to the sky but didn't step completely out of the doorway. "I can't see the red cloud up there anymore," she whispered. "Let's go before it comes back!"

They crept stealthily from the garage. The night was still and hot. Even the leaves on the trees hung motionless on the branches.

Then they heard a dull roar slowly grinding out of the

darkness until it came through like a wind hammer, crashing through the bramble and foliage. They stopped in their tracks and listened as it pounded off the side of the house.

"Brrrian…" The words blew past them. "You must come to me. Come to me. Time is desperate. Soon all will be lost. Come to me now."

"Come to you now? How? The doorway was closed forever. That's what you said."

"You are a ghoooost," exhaled the wind, as it faded into the stillness once again.

"The voice in the wind—it was kind of different, don't you think?" said Cassie.

"I think it was louder, but it must have been Eurus the wind spirit. Who else could it be? Maybe it's because he's really stressed out. How am I supposed to go to him?"

"Well, if he says you can do it then you probably can. Maybe he'll know how to kill off the small red cloud that's stalking us."

"If it's still out here we'd better keep moving," Brian said.

They ran through the streets and down to the dusty road, followed by their elongated shadows. It was quiet except for the sound of the coarse gravel crunching under their feet.

Unbeknownst to Cassie, Brian continued to be impressed by her strength—and not just physical. She was willing to take on the cloud seemingly unafraid, with no whining or fear. And now she kept pace with him with relative ease.

"You can handle anything, can't you?" said Brian.

"I don't know about that," she answered. "I have just learned to take head-on whatever comes at me."

"I'm just glad you're on my side."

"We are good together, you and I."

They shared a penetrating glance that sent sparks into Brian's soul. "This girl is special," he thought. "I know this is the right person for me. I could search for the rest of my life and no one else would even come close."

As they cut down the last road toward home, Brian felt an overwhelming urge to tell Cassie how he felt. He slowed to a trot and reached a gentle hand across her arm. They eased to a stop. Turning to face her, he slid his hands around her slender waist. With his heart pounding and his chest rising and falling, he caught his breath. As he moved his face closer to hers, he could feel her hot breath.

Then their eyes locked, and his words released without thinking. "I…I'm just crazy about you," he said.

She suddenly looked a little shy. But she said, "I know. I've had it bad for you too—ever since the mushrooms."

He leaned in and softly pressed his lips against hers. She dropped the trimmers and wrapped her arms snugly around his neck like she never wanted to let go.

Then Brian felt an ice-cold blob hit his right shoulder. It stuck and began wrapping around his arm. "Agh! What is that?"

Then another hit his calf. It tugged until his foot lifted from the ground. He realized the evil cloud was hovering overhead, dripping softball-size blobs.

Brian raised the shovel over his head for cover just as his toes lost touch with the soil. He heard a ker-ping, and another gooey red blob hit the shovel. It slid off, thumped to the ground, and pooled in the dirt.

Cassie picked up the clippers and franticly cut the thin strands connecting the blobs to the cloud. Sticky drips began raining down on Brian, and she couldn't keep up. Fortunately, the small cloud managed to lift him only a few inches off the ground.

"Don't slow down, just keep cutting!" Brian yelled.

"I'm trying! I'm trying!" Cassie worked fast, and Brian

finally got one foot and then both feet back on the ground.

The severed goo slapped against the soil, instantly soaking in. Before they knew what was happening, the entire cloud began to descend on them, curling around them like a circular curtain. It entered the ground and then bubbled through the soil.

Brian hunched over and tried to rub the feeling back into his limbs numbed from the paralyzing goo. He heard a gurgling noise as the cloud began to sink into the ground. The soil transformed into a bubbling black slime that encircled them. Each moment, the moat of gurgling ooze grew larger.

"We're trapped!" shrieked Cassie, holding the shears defensively.

Brian picked up the shovel and began to heave dirt into the moat, hoping to make an escape path. But as soon as the dirt landed, it sank and dissolved into the bubbling guck.

"It's not working," said Cassie. "We have to make our move quickly."

Dozens of small snakelike tentacles began growing out of the slime, each dripping with goo. They undulated back and forth in the darkness, stretching and reaching for Brian and Cassie.

Cassie feverishly cut the tips of the shiny black tentacles with the shears, as Brian swatted them back with the shovel. Still the sticky moat closed in like a noose getting tighter and tighter.

"We've got to jump across it or we're dead," said Cassie. "We have to go for it now before it gets bigger."

"Okay, let's jump while we still have a chance," yelled Brian.

Having only two steps in which to operate, Cassie sprang like an agile cat. Brian was amazed at the height and length of her flight. There was no question about it; she would easily clear the moat.

Then Brian watched in horror as a tentacle shot out of the slime, like a frog's tongue, and snagged her in midair. The black appendage wrapped itself around her foot and pulled her into the middle of the gurgling ooze. Other tentacles slid smoothly around her waist and limbs and started dragging her under the quicksand-like muck.

Brian was at a loss. He froze for a moment.

"Brian!" she cried out. "Help me!"

He knelt in the dirt, which was quickly vanishing into the ooze, and firmly gripped Cassie's wrist. He leaned back and pulled hard with all his strength; however, his momentum began to falter. Stricken with the fear that Cassie was headed to her death, he threw every bit of physical and mental power he had into wrenching her free. Suddenly, he felt the weight shift his way, and he knew he was beginning to win.

"That's it!" she yelled. "You're doing it."

But his feeling of relief gave way to utter terror when Brian realized he was sinking, too. The muck had expanded into the ground where he knelt. He felt tentacles quickly curl around his calf. Without Brian pulling, Cassie rapidly sank back in.

She was almost gone now. Only the top half of her head was visible. She couldn't even scream because her mouth was submerged. He could only see her crazed eyes.

In the next instant, she sank even deeper.

"Cassie!" he cried out, reaching for her. He could only make out the top of her black hair. Brian struggled, but it only made him sink faster. Cassie was completely gone now, and he was in up to his neck.

He could feel the goo entering his pores. He felt the presence of Leether. With the goo invading every opening in his body he was strangely able to sense the organism's emotions and thoughts. It was so elated at finally catching

43

them that it radiated contentment and excitement.

"Help!" he called out, even though no one was there to hear him. The knowledge that Cassie was gone made living seem less important. Even if he were to survive, he would have the misery of living without her. Now, with goo up to his nose, he tilted his head back and took one final breath before being pulled into the sticky darkness.

The guck entered his ears and nose, and he could feel and taste its bloody, rotting stench. He realized he had very little control of what was happening to him. "But I can decide how I am going to die," he thought. "And I choose to die fighting this thing with my last breath."

Though he believed it was pointless, he began to struggle and thrash wildly. He was going to die his way, and nothing could stop him. He pushed, kicked, and lashed out with all he had left.

Then he felt his aura begin to separate from his body. It withdrew a little at first, and then finally escaped completely and soared out of his slimy tomb. His aura hovered over the bubbling moat for a moment. He remembered the wind spirit's words like music in his head: "You can touch but you cannot be touched."

He willed his aura to dive into the muck. He slipped downward until he felt a slender waist, deep within the black goo. He grabbed on tightly and lifted his beloved Cassie. The slime clung to her like hot taffy but he was able to break free. Carrying her in the air, he laid her at the base of a big tree, a safe distance from the tentacles. Her eyes were wide with terror. After a few anxious moments she took a huge breath. Her pale skin began to regain its pinkish color. She slowly sat up, and then began to cry so hard that her entire body convulsed with each breath.

Satisfied that she'd be okay, Brian's aura went back in

after his own lifeless body. It felt both familiar and odd to drag himself out of the moat. Once his body had been freed, he laid it gently next to Cassie, who was still in tears. Brian's aura entered his body once again, and he sputtered back to life.

When he finally was able to sit up, he noticed the red steamy mist rising from the muck and reforming into a small red cloud. "Can you run?" he coughed.

"I can," she said, as she struggled to her feet. Her head, legs, and torso were entirely covered in black mud—all except the white streaks on her face where her tears had flowed.

"We're almost home. We just have to elude this thing a little longer," Brian said, as he nudged her gently forward. They started running again but this time much faster. "We need to make it to the house before the cloud becomes completely whole again."

They neared their house at the top of a small incline. Cassie stumbled and coughed up vile black crud from her lungs. But onward they ran—two gray shapes moving and blending into the darkness.

When they cleared the side of the house, they sprinted for the back door. Brian threw open the screen and fumbled with the knob. The door was locked. He balled up his fist and banged hard on the door until he saw his mother running toward it in her nightgown. Tommy was just steps behind her.

When she saw the two mud people looking in, she shrieked. Then realizing who they were, she hurriedly let them in. They stepped into the kitchen, dripping black muck onto the wooden floor. The mud began to cake and dry on their skin, changing in color to a powdery gray.

"What in the world happened to you?" asked Mom. "Did the flower witch do this?"

"No, Ma. There is no witch," Brian said, between gasps for air. "It was the red cloud! It went into the ground and formed into gurgling slime and tentacles. We got caught and were pulled down into the muck."

"Holy cow! You could have died," said Tommy. "You should look in the mirror. You even have that black crap in your teeth!"

Cassie spoke up, smearing away muddy tears while she spoke. "We were both swallowed up in darkness. The cloud had us. It was over, and I was dying. Then Brian's aura pulled us out."

"Brian's aura pulled you out?" Tommy shouted.

"We both could easily be dead right now," said Brian "We should have died tonight."

"No one has ever escaped the black ooze," said Cassie.

Mom put a hand on Brian's shoulder, and he hugged her. "I fought it with my last breath, Ma." They embraced and both cried silently together.

Then Brian noticed a broken lamp in the dustpan. "Whoa! What happened to the lamp?"

"It fell off the table—all by itself. I swear I saw you and Grandma together—floating in the living room."

"And you screamed," said Brian.

"Oh, yes I screamed, and in the next instant you were gone."

"If I was actually here, then it was no dream. My aura came back here while I slept."

Cassie smiled. "Does that mean you were really talking to your grandmother?"

"I need time to sort this out," Mom said. "Everything I ever thought was real and true is being challenged by these events."

"Mom! Just look at us. The mud is real, and we are real.

You have to accept it, because like it or not, understand it or not, this is real!"

She looked down and shook her head. "I understand only that I do not understand. I must take it one step at a time. The next thing you two should do is get cleaned up. The kitchen is a mess and you two are a mess. Get in the shower."

"Okay, come on Cassie," Brian said taking her hand.

She smiled and followed.

"One at a time!" Mom yelled down the hall.

"Brian," whispered Cassie. "The kiss was nice, and then everything went to hell. You and me—we have to be more careful. Leether will take every opportunity that we give him."

"No more mistakes," Brian assured her. Then he playfully pushed her into the bathroom.

She good-humoredly flung the door behind her to shut him out, but it banged against Brian's hand. He saw his aura begin to exit through his fingers and penetrate the wood slightly. "Wow! I'm getting less and less locked in. It's like every time I leave my body, the looser I get."

· · ·

After Brian and Cassie showered and put on clean clothes, Mom insisted on a family meeting. As they sat comfortably in the living room, she said, "Okay, I have had a little time to think and I need—no, make that want some answers!"

"Mom," said Brian "I have been thinking, too, and I know what I have to do. I have got to go back through the pond."

"But that windy voice said the doorway was closed forever."

"That voice in the wind is Eurus. He's some kind of wind spirit, and his voice has been telling me to go back. He must be in real trouble. He helped us and got us home, and now I feel that he needs something from me."

"When you threw the crystal into the pond, Brian, didn't that doorway close? This much I am able to understand."

"I know, but I realized that my aura can go where my body can't. When Grandma spoke to me tonight she said, 'The wind is fading.' That can only mean the wind spirit. Eurus is in some big trouble. I need to go and see what I can do for him. And I've got to take the battle to Leether or we will have this nasty cloud hanging over our heads for the rest of our lives. It may be small but it is very capable of killing all of us. Over time, Leether will have the cloud take us out one by one."

"That is a tall order. You could get hurt."

"No, that is the beauty of it. I can't get hurt. As a ghost, I can touch but I can't be touched. Nothing physical can stop me because my aura is not physical. It's life energy. I honestly don't know how the doorway works, but closed or open I should be able to pass through it. I have decided that I'm going back in, and if I'm not back by dawn call the President!"

"Really? The President?" asked Tommy.

"No, but it seemed to fit in with what I was saying. Haven't you always wanted to say that? Now here's the plan for real. I will run into the wall to break my aura free. It would be nice if someone would catch my body before it hits the floor."

"Are you sure you know what you're doing?" asked Tommy.

"I am, in fact, sure that I don't know what I am doing. But I think this is our only real chance to change our situation. Do you want this cloud following us around forever?"

Cassie frowned. "I think you're right—and very brave. But please promise you will come back to me."

He stood and gave both Cassie and his mother a warm embrace.

Tommy stepped in for a group hug.

"Do you have to leave right now?" asked Mom. "It's 2:00 a.m. Can't it wait until morning?"

"I just have this feeling in my gut that it's important for me to get there in a hurry. I think something bad is happening right now, right while we stand here hugging."

"Trust your instincts," said Cassie.

"I promise I will be back in time for breakfast."

"I will have crackling bacon and eggs waiting for you," said Mrs. Hummel.

Brian nodded, and then he stepped back and squared himself with a flat section of living room wall. He took a big breath, as if he were preparing to dive into a pool, and charged the wall. He winced just before he connected, the impact of which dented the drywall and sent two family pictures crashing to the floor.

Brian didn't feel the force of his body ricocheting off the wall, but he did feel the sensation of his aura escaping. He watched with satisfaction as Tommy and Cassie caught his body and laid it gently on the rug.

Free and inspired, he brimmed with confidence as he set out on what he considered to be a noble mission. He was unstoppable. Nothing could touch him. Blending in with the night's summer breeze, he sailed just inches over the tips of the windblown grasses and toward the pond.

# CHAPTER FIVE
# THE GLASSY BALL

Brian hovered over the shimmering pond and stared at his own ghostly reflection in the smooth, mirrored surface. Then he dove into the water without as much as a splash. "Didn't even make a ripple," he chuckled.

When he reached the bottom of the pond he searched for the hole. He saw rocks and weeds but the hole was obscured. "Where is it? It should be directly beneath the raft," he thought. He swished the sandy bottom with his hand. The sand spun in a small watery whirlwind, exposing part of the opening to the tunnel, which he lost no time in entering.

He had never felt more confident or indestructible. "It's amazing how quickly I've gotten used to being a ghost. No need to walk or swim. Things like gravity and walls don't get in my way. The rules of the world don't apply to me anymore. When I think about it, gravity is kind of a dumb rule anyway."

He floated smoothly, having more in common with smoke or a shadow than a young man. He arrived at the membrane, which sealed off the end of the tunnel. Although the membrane was still there it had been transformed. It was no longer gelatinous but had become stiff, black, and glossy.

51

Cutting across the center of the membrane was a thick spidery crack of red goo. "It's like the door shut on the cloud before it got all the way through. Some of the cloud must have stayed in our world, while Leether and the rest of it went back. But this part was trapped in the middle." His outstretched hand slipped easily through the black membrane but found nothing on the other side but dirt. He withdrew his hand and shook his head.

He touched the crack formed by the trapped cloud goo. It was rubbery—almost the same consistency the membrane had been originally. "Maybe this is like when a door is opened a crack." He formed his aura into a thin smoky-looking line and entered the spider crack of goo.

A feeling of ecstasy filled him when he seeped through to the other world. The woods appeared just as he remembered them. The trees were huge and twisted, and the forest floor was a combination of moss and leaves. He regained his humanlike form and floated high above the forest. Gazing down into the valley, he was shocked at how terribly different things had become in just a few days. The Valley of Tears was now a reddish-black swamp. It was filled with fat black tentacles squirming in gurgling red ooze. Crimson mist popped from the bubbling slime, and red clouds dotted the sky. "What has happened here? Things look really, really bad!"

Brian let himself drift upward, like an escaping balloon, until he could see over the entire mountain range encircling the valley. Moving on, he sailed over the ghastly castle and mountain peaks. He followed the same route he remembered taking during his last visit to the wind spirit's tower. He passed over the camp of the hell beasts and gazed at the blasting pit of fire, and then he flew over the Mushroom Forest and the steamy snake-filled river.

Swooping in low, he tracked the winding river right up to the sandy shore of the wind spirit's tiny island. He sighed when he spotted Eurus's castle tower with its shimmering glass dome. The tower jutted proudly from the middle of the island.

Brian smiled. "It's so much easier now. I've got this!" He sailed through the dark thorns and chattering blackbirds that surrounded the tower. "Nothing can stop me, and I have nothing to fear." Feeling free he spread his arms and soared like a great winged bird. He entered the tower like a flicker of light through the glass dome. He hovered vertically, just inches from the white, marble iris embedded in the floor. Completely transparent, he turned slowly, looking for any movement that would disrupt the stillness of the quiet hexagon-shaped room.

Everything was as he remembered it. There were rows and rows of bookcases and several large doors in the room. Huge frozen statues stood in the corners, each holding dripping candles. The grotesque creatures looked as if they could thaw out at a moment's notice to lunge at him.

He drifted toward the desk in front of the bookcases. "This is new," he said, picking up a square black box that sat on top of a disorganized scattering of papers. He opened the box and saw a glassy ball. Something was moving inside it. He could just make out an ashen, panic-stricken face looking back at him with its palms pressed against the glass.

All of a sudden Brian felt something tug at his back. "That shouldn't happen," he thought. "An outside force can't affect my ghostly form."

He was taken so off guard that he didn't react at first. But as he turned he saw a person standing in the middle of the iris pointing a long clear tube at him.

The draw was sudden and overpowering, and before he

could clearly understand what was happening, Brian found himself being sucked into the tube. He dropped the black box. His shape twisted and swirled toward the tube. Within seconds, his entire aura was trapped inside it.

Two hands quickly blocked both ends of the tube. The palms pressed against either side and began compressing it. Then the large hands massaged the warm transparent glass, and formed the tube into a ball.

He was horrified and stunned by the sound of a powerful voice. It had so much bass that it shook the air. "Justice will be done for Nimbus!"

"Leether!"

The cloud priest held up the glass ball. "I've got you, my slippery boy," Leether said with great exuberance. "Do you recall the last time we met? You put a smoking hole in my back. And ever since it has been a painful reminder of what I am meant to do to you. You are so foolish. Don't you know that even smoke can be trapped? You are securely contained in my hands. You were so easy to manipulate, I am almost disappointed."

Though Brian struggled to regain his shape, he remained a swirling mass of confused smoke inside the glassy ball.

Leether's face and red eyes appeared distorted as Brian peered at him through the concave curve of his transparent prison. Leether held up the ball and gave an elated cry of victory. "AAAAAEEEEEAAH!"

Brian wanted to cry out but couldn't form the words or make a sound. "I am completely helpless. I will be trapped here for all eternity." In utter frustration he let go with a silent scream that only he could hear in his own mind.

"Your wind spirit Eurus has been beaten, too," Leether said with venom. "He crossed me for the last time when he helped you escape. Finishing him was like removing a splintered thorn. Nothing can stop the will of Nimbus.

"It was easy to destroy his body while his aura was off to who knows where. Then I found this little trick marked in one of his books. I surprised him when he returned and caught his aura in a glass energy ball. Quite a cute trick, don't you think? I will eventually learn all his secrets. I had no idea there was so much I could take from him. I even learned how to send my voice to be carried off like the howling wind.

"Your body back home can wither and die because I have the part of you that I want. I will bring you and Eurus to the tower altar, and I will call the cloud down to consume you both. What a glorious ceremony we shall have! And in time I will take your family too, one by one. My little cloud will bide its time. It will continue to grow larger and stronger as it lies in wait for them. This is a glorious day!"

Leether turned his head and sniffed. "What's that stink? Filthy hell beasts! Those overgrown horned toads must have followed me here! Six hundred pounds of aggravation packed into each one of them."

Brian spotted thick black smoke pouring in under the closed door.

Leether's head snapped back, and he saw it, too. "What's this now?" he growled with outrage.

A loud concussion suddenly rocked the room, and the walls burst into bright yellow flames. Leether hastily set Brian's ball on the desk.

Brian watched, mesmerized, as Leether pulled his twisted staff out of the sheath slung over his back, raised it high in the air, and faced the large door.

The golden knob on the top of the staff began to emit red vapor from small vented holes. "Vapor vapid, a spiritless brume… Well, come on! If you want me, here I am, you horned devils."

With a loud bang, the doorway exploded into shattered boards and splinters. A swarm of fierce hell beasts crashed into the room. They were muscular-looking reptilian apes. Each one was at least eight feet tall with the face and skin of a horned toad. The insane herd of beasts tore through the room in an angry rampage.

Leether thrust his staff toward the ceiling. "Rufescent phantom!" he shouted.

A beast lunged at him and knocked the scepter from Leether's hand. The golden knob broke loose and flew across the room. Red goo splattered as it clanked against the wall. The beast struggled with Leether; the other hell beasts joined in.

The smoke grew thicker and blacker. Brian felt a pulsating rhythm, as hot waves of yellow flames obscured his view. He pushed his energy from side to side and was eventually able to tip and then rock the ball until it started to roll. Soon, he was able to move to it toward the edge of the desk.

"This might be the last chance I get to break out of here," he thought. He built up momentum until the ball rolled smoothly off the edge and plummeted. His stomach lifted, as if he were riding a roller coaster and had just hit the first big drop. Just before striking the floor, the ball landed in the open palms of two thick, bumpy hands. Dingy yellowed claws closed around him.

"GRARRAAA!" A huge lumpy beast grunted in exaltation. All Brian could see were flashes of yellow and red and then black again, as the fire grew.

Just as Leether stretched out to grab the black box, Brian saw a beast backhand him, sending him flying across the room. "The beasts are winning this one," Brian thought.

Flaming bookcases tumbled, and the glass dome over the room shattered from the heat. Chards rained down making a sound like wind chimes in a hurricane. When Brian saw blue sky and sun he realized the beast was carrying him out a window and down the side of the tower.

"These beasts aren't here to save me," he thought. "They destroy for the pure enjoyment of destruction. I can only hope he drops this thing and I break out."

The beast jumped the last thirty feet to the ground, which shook the trees around them. It ran in a straight line through a thicket of sharp black thorns, never slowing or moving to avoid them. It took no notice of the thorns impaling its skin and sending green blood dripping over its lumpy scaled body. Branches snapped off, and blackbirds jumped from the trees, cawing and swirling overhead.

The beast never slowed as it ran headlong into the river. Its immense weight held it solidly to the bottom, and it ran smoothly along the riverbed, sending schools of fish spinning in its wake. Soon the great beast climbed out of the river on the opposite bank. Hundreds of huge beasts yelped and charged out of the water with it.

Brian heard a loud roar and watched, through the beast's fingers, as the castle tower collapsed into a huge rolling ball of flames. A bright yellow mushroom-shaped plume of smoke rose hundreds of feet into the air.

Brian's form was so shaken that he didn't know his head from his feet. "How do I get out of this one?" he wondered. "These monsters love to fight and are afraid of nothing. I've been saved from Leether, but I could actually be worse off, if that's possible."

The beast clenched the ball firmly and started to sprint through the forest. It was so strong and fast that to Brian the woods looked like a green blur. It ran without slowing for what seemed like hours.

Finally, the beast broke through the trees. And after

clearing the crest of a hill it trotted into the camp of the hell beasts. The camp, shaped like an oblong bowl, had a huge pit of fire roaring at one end. Brian estimated that it was twenty feet wide and appeared to connect with an underground volcanic system. Fire belched violently from the pit as immense heat escaped from underground pressure. A shadowy forest grew at the opposite end of the bowl.

"I remember this place," Brian thought. "This is what Ebil called the Pit of Despair."

Brian's lumpy savior slowed to a stop, as many other panting beasts cowered around him. Brian's beast held up the glassy ball as if to show off its great prize. The other beasts cheered wildly.

Brian got a good look at the creature when it held the ball up to its snakelike yellow eyes. Its skin was mostly green with shiny blue colors running through its scales, similar to the coloring of a fish. Brian decided to call him Greenie.

Greenie's nostrils seemed bigger than necessary, and he had several large horns on top of his head and shoulders. As if a few horns were not enough, he also had many, smaller ones, like a horned toad.

It was hard to decipher the expression on Greenie's face, but Brian thought it was a smile. The beast nuzzled the globe with his moist snout and sniffed curiously. A greasy smear of warm snot stuck and slid down the glassy surface.

"Garrahhh!" cried Greenie, as he held up the ball.

A slightly larger beast with red eyes moved in on them. Its stride spoke of dominating confidence. Brian guessed Red Eye was some type of beastly leader.

"Gruuuta!" barked Red Eye. The beast held out its hand, obviously wanting Greenie to relinquish the globe.

Greenie held it out, at first, and then changed his mind. He hugged the ball against his face and licked it with a sticky forked tongue. Saliva dripped from the globe.

"Gruuuta!" growled Red Eye, and he moved closer, his hand firmly extended.

Greenie tightened his grip and moved away. This sent shrills and clamoring through the crowd of beasts watching.

Red Eye, who was larger, lunged forward and grabbed the ball. A massive tug-of-war ensued. The fight was so violent and loud that Brian could only assume it was a battle to the death.

The beastly spectators went into a frenzy, jumping uncontrollably and screaming indiscernible words. With the monsters tangled in a dance of death it was hard for Brian to see what was going on.

Suddenly, Red Eye grabbed Greenie by the throat and threw the beast backward toward the fire pit.

Greenie stumbled but never let go of his glass prize. Brian could feel the heat from the flames, which roared from below.

The red-eyed leader lunged at Greenie and tackled him with such force that Greenie lost his grip on the ball. Greenie was pinned face down in the dirt.

Brian felt himself drop to the ground. In horror, he realized that his glassy prison was rolling toward the blasting flames. He managed to get a glance at Greenie just as Red Eye bit a mouthful of meat from the smaller beast's shoulder.

Red Eye looked up with flesh and blood dripping from his jowls. "Arrcha!" he yelled, as he noticed the ball getting dangerously close to the fire. Red-Eye dove forward and snatched the globe before it reached the flames. He lay stretched out on the ground as he cradled the ball. He rolled onto his back and held it up, turning it slowly, as if marveling at its beauty.

From Brian's newfound vantage point, he saw Greenie

leap high into the air and land full force onto the leader's chest, with his knees. Greenie reared his head back and opened his large jowls. Lunging forward, he chomped off Red Eye's fingertips with an enormous bite, thus bringing them and the glassy ball into his mouth.

From inside Greenie's mouth, Brian heard Red Eye scream. And then all sounds became muffled as Greenie began to chew.

# CHAPTER SIX

# THROUGH THE EYES OF THE BEAST

Numb with shock, Brian frantically wondered what was going to become of him.

The beast swallowed with a loud gulp. But instead of sliding into Greenie's belly Brian felt himself being absorbed into the beast's entire body—even into his consciousness.

Gradually, Brian began making out fuzzy images. Then the images sharpened. When it all came into focus, he realized that he was actually looking through the monster's eyes.

"I am locked in!" he thought. "I am locked into the monster's body!"

It was such an odd sensation. At once he noticed that his vision was sharper than ever—in fact, all his senses were greatly enhanced.

Greenie's thoughts and feelings, though not in words, were clear to Brian. Greenie was passionate about destroying Red Eye. He and the red-eyed leader had a history. They had been combatants before, with neither of them ever having a clear win.

The frenzy increased, and the jubilant crowd of beasts

grew larger as Greenie and Red Eye circled each other, slowly measuring and anticipating the other's first move. One of the beasts threw Red Eye a large curved sickle. He caught it with one swipe of his hand, a tight-lipped reptilian smile crossing his face. But his eyes were angry and hot, bubbling over with rage.

Gripping the sickle with his bloody stubs, the beast seemed to laugh. Then he jumped forward while taking a wide swing.

Brian, who was now one with Greenie, tried in vain to jump back. The sickle sliced deep into his side, but his skin was so thick it didn't penetrate the muscle.

Red Eye pulled and tugged but could not free the blade.

Brian held the base of the handle as blood began to ooze from the gash. His emotions began to combine with those of the creature. He never felt so powerful and angry in all his life. He was awed by his new strength. With his superior brainpower he was able to dominate the beast's thoughts.

Suddenly Brian realized something else. "My senses are amazing. I can smell blood, sense fear, and even taste the smoke in the air. I can distinguish each individual sound in the forest. I can even hear the thumping of each beast's heart. And I honestly understand what these monsters are saying!

"Maybe I can outsmart old Red Eye," he thought. On impulse, Brian made a gurgling noise and then fell onto his back, as if he were dying.

Red Eye began hopping up and down wildly in a victory dance. A roar erupted from the crowd. The excitement multiplied as they chanted and encouraged their leader to throw Greenie into the fire, which was apparently the customary way to conclude a fight.

Red Eye cautiously leaned in and sniffed to see if Greenie was still alive. Brian held his breath and tried to slow the loud pounding of his heart. He could sense the beast within him crying out. It wanted to follow its instincts to move, react, and attack. Brian suppressed the urge, but it took all the mental strength he could muster. "If I can keep slowing my heartbeat, maybe the beast will think I am near death."

Red Eye cocked his thorny head to one side to listen, and then he slowly reached down and gave Greenie a poke with his good hand. At that moment, Brian reared back his legs and, with both feet, kicked Red Eye in the ribs, causing him to stumble backward. The surprised beast flailed his arms as he tried to catch his balance.

Brian quickly kicked himself up to his feet and winced in pain as he pried the sickle blade loose from his bloody abdomen.

Red Eye tried to regain his balance. Finally, he caught himself just one step from the searing fire.

Brian sprang forward, took the sickle with both his hands, and blasted his opponent across the chest. Red Eye reeled backward into the wall of fire, and was engulfed in sizzling flames. In a moment, he was gone, vanishing into the white-hot wall of fire with no more than a puff of black smoke.

Brian awaited the reaction from the hostile crowd. The beasts must have wanted Red-Eye to win; after all, they had given him a weapon. To Brian's surprise, the beasts couldn't have been more delighted by the sudden turn of events. They roared and danced wildly. He was grabbed and lifted overhead by the large crowd as they chanted, "Garrah! Garrah!"

"I must be the big dog now," Brian thought.

He could feel Greenie's brain working slowly, like a big slow gear inside of a fast-moving clock. Brian knew the creature understood that they shared the same body. The creature rejoiced at the victory—his emotions somehow intertwining with Brian's thoughts.

It was then that Brian realized he was now the new leader of the most awful creatures anyone could ever imagine. He was carried around the camp, while the beasts threw their heads back and bellowed so loudly little animals tumbled off their branches.

"Everything is happening to me so fast," Brian thought. "I have become this horrible green beast, and if that isn't bad enough, these monsters expect me to lead them. I am cursed. What if I can never escape this body? Maybe I can break my aura free from this beast anytime I want."

With his claws, Brian motioned to be set down. The beasts gently put him back on his feet. Then he broke into a run with surprising quickness. He headed toward the forest on the other side of the clearing, zeroing in on a mature tree. It was big enough to wrap his arms around, so certainly it would stop him. He ran at it hard. Picking up speed he slammed into the tree with a loud crack. The tree creaked then crashed to the ground with leaves pluming into the air.

But Brian's aura stayed locked in. "Grrraah!" he howled in frustration, as he clenched his fists. He felt numbness from the impact but no pain, at least not pain as a person experiences it.

"These beasts have the strength of a bulldozer!" he muttered to himself.

The beasts all cheered. Many followed suit and began running into trees of their own, sending them toppling to the ground. A cheer sounded each time a tree fell, and the beasts jumped around with excitement. Brian stood bewildered in the middle of the madness. He watched in wonder as tree after tree succumbed to the beasts' strength.

Eventually the beasts began to tire of the tree-tipping

game. Little by little they swaggered back into camp as a cool darkness began to settle over the Pit of Despair.

Some settled by the fire, while others scratched in the dirt like dogs.

"I control the body of a scary eight-foot monster," Brian thought. "If Leether survived the fire and is still stalking me, I could wipe him out with one backhand. The other beasts easily knocked him around at the tower, and they had no intelligent plan whatsoever.

"Leether was probably killed in the fire. No—he's alive—I can feel it. Ever since that bubbling guck got into my pores I can sense him somehow. Yeah, he still haunts me, but so what? I should take the battle to him. After all, I am the leader of one hundred and fifty of the meanest and most disgusting monsters you would ever want to see. But then who would want to see anything that looks like me?"

Brian laughed at the thought, and it came out as an enormous "GRRAHA-HA!"

"Garraw," barked a beast. Then a dozen or so beasts ran up and over the top of the hill in a tight pack, leaving the camp.

Brian, beginning to understand some of their basic language, understood that they were going to hunt for dinner. He shuddered at the thought. "I can't even begin to guess what they might bring back."

Brian could feel the strength of Greenie's heart thumping in his chest. He had toppled a good-sized tree with little effort. He looked at his bumpy arms covered with protective scales. He held up his lumpy hands and looked at the thick claws jutting out sharply from each finger. "I have thumbs," he thought. "I guess I'm some type of reptilian-ape-beast thing. When you think about it, I'm almost humanoid. I have arms, legs, and feet." He looked behind him. "What's this—a tail? Oh, and I have a tail."

Slowly, he became aware that his skin was shrinking. He was getting skinnier. "My skin puffed out while I was excited. When I get stressed, my skin must puff up bigger— like a blowfish—for protection. That explains why the sickle didn't cut into my vital organs." He looked at the cut left by the blade. The deep gash looked severe, but the pain was just a minor discomfort.

A lumpy, rather toxic-smelling beast approached him with a large handful of sticky red clay. It grabbed his wrist and lifted his arm up with one hand, and then pressed the clay into the wound on his side and one on his shoulder.

"Wow, a nice gesture," Brian thought. "Maybe I have misjudged these creatures."

The beast actually seemed to give him a slight smile before going off to cover itself in a dark blanket of dirt.

• • •

Twenty minutes later Brian heard the shrill squeal of a razorback hog. A small gerbit raced through the camp. Without warning, several hell beasts crashed through the brush with little porkers under each arm. The pigs were making a terrible racket and squirming fiercely but could not free themselves.

"Are they going to eat the gerbits?" Brian wondered.

A beast with gray spikes jutting from his chin was the last one to come over the hill. He was dragging a man by one foot and had a small pig under his free arm.

"Oh, no! This is what they got us for dinner?" Then Brian's fear elevated to horror when he recognized the man. It was his crazy old friend, Ebil. The little porker was the very gerbit they had saved from drowning.

Brian growled in beast lingo to demand Ebil's release. Saliva streamed from his jaws and ran down his chin.

Gray Beard glared at him in defiance.

Ebil's shoulders kicked up dust as he was dragged along, but he looked unafraid. He had his hands interlaced behind his head as if he were relaxing and enjoying the ride.

Brian clearly understood the beasts' crude language, and Greenie's thoughts kept mixing with his. Strangely, it was not an adverse relationship where they each struggled for control. It was the truest form of teamwork, with Brian having the upper hand in brain strength. One animal and one man both teaming up to control one very powerful creature.

Gray Beard brought Ebil and the pig toward the fire. Several beasts busied themselves by chopping large bamboo poles with curved sickles and shaping the ends into points.

Brian winced. "I hope they aren't going to stick them with those poles. Could I get there in time to stop it? Would I even be able to stop it?"

"Garratt!" Brian barked.

When Gray Beard still paid him no mind, Brian felt consumed by an irrepressible rage. He ran and leaped fifteen feet into the air, descending with his claws and teeth exposed. He dug into Gray Beard's back with such ferocity and savagery that he shocked himself. He realized the unthinkable horror he was now capable of.

Gray Beard slammed face first into the dirt, which allowed Ebil and the gerbit to break free.

Brian bit down and tasted Gray Beard's blood as it filled his mouth—and he liked it. "What have I become?" he wondered. "I'm out of control!"

Brian kept Gray Beard pinned down in the dirt as he looked to make sure Ebil and the gerbit were safe.

Ebil casually sat near the fire and warmed his hands. The

gerbit trotted over to Ebil and nuzzled under his arm for safety.

Ebil scratched the top of the gerbit's rubbery nose and smiled at Brian. "Your eyes give you away bumble…it has to beeee. Bodies are only vessels; I see who is inside there through the windows of your eyes. It is the inner being that knows the truth and the lies. It is the inner being that lives when the body dies."

"He knows me!" Brian thought. "He can see my inner soul."

"Hi, Ebil," Brian tried to say, but it came out, "Hatta Garrbta." When he spoke, his big forked tongue lashed out and flopped clumsily to the side. He sucked it back in like a loose strand of spaghetti.

Ebil laughed. "Hatta Garrrbta? Reality and dreams, here's where they differ. In reality, you are one scary nightmare."

Gray Beard struggled to stand, but Brian kept him pinned. He was afraid to let him up. "Now what do I do with this angry guy?" he wondered.

Several end pieces of cut bamboo had been left lying on the ground near Ebil. He picked up two hollow pieces and struck them against a third. "Hmm, music," he said.

He sat Indian style and began to play a thumping rhythm on pieces of hollow bamboo while he sang: "Two peas in a pod, two of one mind not affected by time. La, la, la, we all fall down in the bubbling slime! Ha, ha, ha." While he played, Ebil bobbed his head to the beat, and the little gerbit did figure eights. "Ber-at-tat… Ber-at-ta-tat-tat."

The beasts ceased what they were doing and took interest. Many of them rose to their scaly feet and approached Ebil.

Brian realized that Gray Beard had stopped struggling. "I think my point has been made," Brian thought. He let up on the pressure and climbed off the spiky-chinned beast. Gray Beard slowly got to his feet. He crouched, as if preparing to lunge and attack. Then he cracked his neck and looked coldly into Brian's eyes.

"He's even uglier than a horned toad," Brian thought. He could almost taste the anger emanating from the gruesome, thorny creature.

"Gaarrta!" growled the beast as he stepped right up to Brian's face. "Peraahta!" Spittle hit Brian's scaly cheeks and hung like gooey icicles from his chin.

Brian shoved Gray Beard back so hard it almost sent him tumbling into the flaming pit. The beast quickly regained his balance with one arm. He spun on his planted hand and quickly exited through the crowd of beasts, who were dancing clumsily to Ebil's drumming.

Ebil glanced around the clearing and continued his mad ramblings while he played. "The Pit of Despair; the point of no return—will I escape or stay here to burn? They will want to kill me a lot and then roast me hot. Maybe I should look at the bright side—you can't be killed if you've already died!"

He laughed and playing faster and faster while beasts danced around him. "Soon Snow will come and the sky will turn red, and Brian will try to eat someone's head! Ah ha, ha, ha."

Brian watched the little gerbit, who was content just to be by Ebil's side. It snorted and snuggled in the soft dirt next to him. "I can't stand by and let the beasts start eating Ebil or even the gerbits," he thought.

Brian watched as the beasts surrounded and taunted the frightened gerbits, who huddled in a tight circle. "If I ordered the beasts to let them go, they would probably mutiny and throw me in the fire."

A large crowd of beasts continued to dance in a goofy spinning fashion. Their celebration led them around the fire pit. Every so often one would lose its balance or get pushed into the pit, where it disintegrated.

Brian looked on in wonder. "These beasts are truly evil. I can't lose sight of that. Life has no value to them. I guess that when your own life has no value there is no concern for anyone else's life either. What's worse is that they are quick to anger, and they love a fight."

Brian felt the burning anger deep within him. Until now, he had never felt emotions so intensely.

Ebil slowed his rhythm and, like toys winding down, the monsters began to sway and move slowly back to the holes they had dug for themselves in the dirt.

Brian strolled over and sat down next to his old friend.

Ebil stopped playing and laughed, "You are on the dark side now. How does it feel to be in the thick scaly skin? But don't worry, you are in need. For what is light without dark? Good without bad? Where would cold be without hot? Big is not big without small; strong without weak. Even fast is not so fast without slow. It will change you, don't you know?"

Exhausted from the day, Brian leaned back and lay in the dirt as Ebil talked on and on. "If there is no contrast, there is no significance. It is a paradox that could fool even the cleverest fox…I mean, I mean…if you have everything, you have nothing. Yes, that's it! If you have nothing, you will appreciate everything—that is until you get everything which, as I said, is nothing."

Brian began to drift off to a much-needed sleep. Even though he had stopped giving Ebil his full attention, it was comforting to hear him ramble on.

"The sun never feels as warm as when you have clawed your way out of the cold darkness," Ebil continued. "And, may I say, it was never so cold or dark as it is for you now. Even if you were able to climb back into your own skin, everything stacks up. Every smooth thing cracks up. Every tower eventually falls; everything has a last curtain call. When you are cut, you will earn a scar. If you are made lame, you will not go far. Every experience makes changes, and your outer-self rearranges."

Finally, sleep overtook Brian. But after a few moments, he was jarred back to consciousness with a thundering Ka-Boom! Boom! Boom! Ka-Boom! Boom! Boom!

"Gargon!" yelped Ebil. By the time Brian roused from his short slumber, the gargon was already upon them. The ground shook with such force that the hell beasts were knocked off their feet. A gargon twenty feet high erupted from the woods and into the clearing. It scooped a beast into its mouth.

The gargon looked much like a mythical dragon but it had no wings and didn't spit fire. It was a prehistoric-looking eating machine.

But the reaction at the camp was one of joy, not panic. Quickly the beasts swarmed around the mammoth gargon, leaping on to it as it spun around biting as many as it could with each chomp.

Brian saw Gray Beard leap onto the gargon's tail and work his way up its back. Using his needle sharp claws Gray Beard dug in for a wild ride. The gargon turned his head as far back as he could, but couldn't quite get his fangs into Gray Beard.

Gray Beard sank his claws deep into the gargon's hide and began to climb up its neck. Once on top of the creature's slippery head, he steadied himself by holding onto the gargon's pointy ears.

The gargon spun, bucking like a bull. It shook off all the beasts, except for Gray Beard.

Flexing his yellow claws, Gray Beard dove down, and dug

them into the gargon's eyes. Blood squirted and the creature let out a shrill, piercing scream. It shook its head frantically, but Gray Beard never let go.

The blinded beast stumbled, and Gray Beard scrambled back on top of its head, yanking hard on its right ear. With this maneuver, Gray Beard managed to steer the creature toward the fire pit. Now blind, the gargon unknowingly ran headlong toward the fire. Gray Beard jumped from its head and rolled away, just as the gargon fell across the belching flames. Smoke bellowed from the pit, as the fire consumed it.

"Eraarraa!" cheered the excited beasts.

Then the feeding frenzy began. The crazed beasts clamored like wild dogs as they tore off chunks of the gargon with their razor sharp teeth.

It was obvious to Brian that Gray Beard had just placed himself in a position of prominence.

The gerbits, now unafraid of becoming the next meal, joined in the feast. They darted between the beasts' legs, grabbing tidbits of gargon flesh.

Brian found himself tearing off a large piece of smoking flesh with his teeth, too. He chomped at the savory meat.

"You are the beast now," said Ebil, walking up behind him. "Welcome to the shallows—darkness and cold, too. I feel the chill, and the demon is you."

Brian wondered if he could form any discernible words, if he concentrated hard enough. He opened his heavy jaws, but it felt more like prying opening a mousetrap than getting ready to speak. "Ieeee geerrunder staaann," Brian managed to say.

Ebil laughed. "You gerunderstan?"

"Slerzard Razzzz wherr?"

"Where are Slizard and Razz? Um, well, they don't live

in tunnels under the forest floor. Slizard and Razz and most of the Thorks could be no more. Those who have not sunk into the goo have scattered across the land like rats with no clue. All has been lost. Thorks were flushed out of the ground like bumbles. The red cloud of death entered the tunnels. They were unaware, unearthed, unnerved— everyone tattered, fractured and scattered. Nimbus and Leether were too strong, too smart, too evil. I fear it can only be stopped by itself. With no home base, and Nimbus giving chase, I climbed over the mountain. After escaping my foe I ran into Snow."

"Ran into snow?" thought Brian. "There is no snow. It sounds like Slizard may be dead, and who knows what happened to the rest of the Thorks?"

He closed his eyes. His large shoulders sank with despair. He no longer felt like eating. Dropping his head, he walked over to the nearest dirt hole. He bent down and scratched a little more dirt out like a dog, then lay down and covered himself with the loose soil, as he had seen the other beasts do. He tried to relax, but there was still a lot of commotion by the pit as the beasts continued to gorge themselves on the smoldering gargon.

"I am in so deep," he thought. "How am I going to get out of this?" His thick and lumpy skin felt like a suit of armor that he could never take off.

"What is happening at home?" he wondered. "It's so far away. I don't know how I will ever be able to see it again. I promised Cassie I would be back by breakfast. I'm not sure what day this even is, but I know breakfast came and went a long time ago. How long will my body back at home last without my aura?"

He noticed Gray Beard kneeling, as he sharpened a bamboo pole with the edge of the sickle blade. "And with everything else, I have Mr. Popular Toad Face plotting against me. What are the positives? I have never been in a better position to fight Leether. No medieval army could ever beat these monsters."

Brian's eyes rolled back, and he dozed off as he pondered his next move. That night Brian's dream mixed with the subconscious mind of the beast. He dreamed as the beast would dream:

His huge muscular body ran with ease through the woods. It felt wonderful to move so fast. He saw something sprinting ahead of him. As he approached, he could see it more clearly. The something was trying to outrun him, as he pursued. He leaped over rocks and toppled trees, while he steadily gained ground. Then it struck him that he was chasing a man. An angry fire burned in his gut, and his mouth began to salivate.

He was gradually awakened, not by a noise but by a distinctive smell. It was human. Before even opening his eyes he sensed it was a woman and two men. He could smell their sweat and hear the vibrating pulse of blood pushing through their veins. He remained still, and just listened.

Their hearts raced. They were only a few feet behind him now. He heard the woman whisper, "The beasts sleep so soundly when they have full bellies. But you've got to come quickly. We can only save you if we hurry."

"Why would I leave?" Brian heard Ebil say.

"Are you crazy?"

"Is that a problem?"

A man with a gravelly voice whispered, "Skhat, I told you we shouldn't have tried to get him. It's way too risky."

Brian heard the sound of a slap. He rolled over and opened his catlike eyes. A short Knight in rusty black armor had latched onto Ebil's wrist and was pulling him to his feet. There was also another Black Knight with him—and a middle-aged woman. Brian's beastly eyes made contact with the shorter knight's pink little eyes. The knight froze in terror like a little rabbit, but never let go.

Brian reached up from where he lay and clung onto Ebil's other arm. He pulled him away from the pale-looking knight in rusty armor.

"He won't be going with you," Brian tried to say, but it came out all garbled. "Womba gerra-doo."

The rusty knight looked like an albino. He had long, white hair that hung out the bottom of his spiked helmet. The taller knight had such a full bushy beard that it puffed out of his helmet on all sides. Brian instantly found this odd, as any knight he had ever seen was well groomed, with armor buffed to a black shine. The woman had straight hair, black with several wide streaks of silver. She wore an ankle-length coat covered in scales.

"Run!" she yelled in a panic. The three of them raced through camp zigzagging around the sleeping beasts.

Brian sprang to his feet and lunged forward, catching the woman and the pale knight by the backs of their necks. He lifted them off the ground. Their feet dangled while they trembled wide-eyed with fear. Brian shook the pale knight, and he dropped his sword in the dirt.

The knight with the bushy beard was very spry; it appeared he would escape. He made it up the rise then took a running leap through the small saplings on the outskirts of the clearing. With all the turmoil, the beasts started to awaken.

Several growling beasts charged out of camp after him, like a pack of wolves. They left the clearing with so much force that they left behind a trail of tumbling trees.

Then Brian heard a muffled scream. It was silenced before the words had completely formed.

"Skhat is dead!" the woman cried.

Brian held her closer to examine her face. Through her contorted expression and her tears, he saw there was something strangely familiar about her. "Where have I seen her before?" he wondered. "If these are Leether's knights, then where is Leether? Why were they here? To save Ebil? It was quite heroic of them, really. It doesn't add up. Why would Leether want Ebil rescued?"

"Don't worry, Sarah," said the albino knight, "Skhat will not be alone."

"Why?" Sarah asked.

"We are soon to join him."

"Snow, you have always been here for me," she said, as they dangled together from Brian's large hands. "I fear you're right. We've gotten out of many a bad fix, but if ever it was over—I think it is now."

The woman craned her neck to look back into Brian's eyes. She must have seen a glimmer of something that made her hopeful. "You don't want to hurt me, do you?" She forced an uncomfortable smile. "There is something about this one; I swear there is a thinking mind in there."

"What do you mean?"

"I'm telling you that this beast's eyes are different. They look aware and intelligent." She twisted her neck around even more for a better look. "I am Sarah, and this is Snow."

"Mind or no mind," said Snow, "we live only until it gets hungry."

"Don't be so sure," Sarah said. She reached up and grabbed onto Brian's fingers. "Mr. Green monster, you are hurting my neck. Could you please put us down?"

Brian would have smiled, but as a beast he could not completely form that expression. He set Sarah and Snow back onto their feet.

Sarah rubbed the soreness from her neck, and Snow retrieved his sword from the ground.

Gray Beard roughly bumped Brian to one side and yanked Sarah and Snow away from him by their arms, much like a mother would pull aside a bad child. Brian tensed but did not react. He fought his inner hostility so he could see what Grey Beard was going to do next, before deciding on his next move.

Two beasts joined Gray Beard in picking up the bamboo poles that had been cut. Gripping each pole hand over hand they spiked the ends into the ground. The dry soil made a puff sound as it succumbed to their strength. Gray Beard and friends began building a circle of poles around Sarah and Snow. Several grunting gerbits were put in the circle with them. While they worked, another beast slammed melon-sized balls of sap onto the top of each pole. The work was done with clockwork precision.

"The beasts must have performed this ritual hundreds of times," Brian thought.

Next, Gray Beard lit each ball of sap with a torch, imprisoning Sarah, Snow, and the gerbits inside the small, flaming circle.

Brian cocked his head in wonder. "What will be next? I hate to think about it. Will I spend the rest of my life with these cannibalistic monsters? And what if I lose control of the beast inside my head and do something awful?"

Ebil remained by the fire twirling his hair and humming random notes. Brian knelt next to him and spoke quietly. His words were garbled in growls but it was the best he could manage. "Ebil, listen to me," he tried to say.

"No, listen to me," said Ebil. "Black spikes will wash over the rise; the red sky will drown out the cries. Think quickly or everyone dies."

"Yeah, okay—whatever you say, just get ready to run," Brian said with his beastly tongue. It came out in growls, but Ebil seemed to understand. "I'm going to order the beasts to let everyone go, and I'm going to do it now."

"Now? When is now? If it hasn't happened yet how can it be now? How long does it take before the present vanishes into the past?" Ebil began rubbing his temples, as if perplexed. "The past and future have no end, but the present moves like a bubble in the wind."

Brian began again. He concentrated hard and formed words slowly with much labor. "Ebil, if you gunderstan, nod your head."

Ebil looked up at him and nodded with an impish grin.

Brian wanted to say that releasing the woman and knight would lead to chaos. "All hell will break loose, and when it does, you get yourself out of here. Run as fast as you can for as long as you can." But when he said it his words were completely indiscernible. Ebil nodded and put his hand on Brian's lumpy face. "Good monster," Ebil said with a toothy, crooked smile.

Brian understood that the ring of flaming poles were like a line in the sand. It formed a cage that could not hold Sarah and the knight physically, but if they stepped out they would be brutally killed. Brian stood and moved toward the captives.

The albino knight trembled when Brian caught his gaze. He was the short and stocky variety Brian had become accustomed to seeing in this world, but he had odd pink eyes that almost glowed from inside the tarnished spiked helmet.

The woman was about 5' 6" and slender. She was not built short and thick like a Thork or a Tred. She wore a black leather vest and black shorts. Her ankle length coat appeared to have been made from the scaly skin of hell beasts. She was barefooted.

Obviously trying to conjure up his nerve, the albino knight spoke. "Hey there, ugly, are we to be your dinner? Free us and I will show you where the Black Knights are hiding. Don't let this old armor fool you; we are fighting them, too. There's a huge army ramping up for reasons unknown. We were eluding them when Ebil seemingly let himself get captured by the beasts. We can team up and help each other. What do you say? There are a lot of them, enough to feed all of you for years. Just let us go and we work togeth… you don't understand a thing, do you—you stupid piece of stinking evil. Why am I wasting my breath?"

"Grrrrraaaaaa!" growled Brian. Unintentionally he exposed his vicious teeth. Unnerved, the knight stepped back.

"With beasts there's always fight and fright," said Ebil. "Most of the time it happens all the time."

Growling and snorting, several beasts wandered over to harass the two newest captives.

"This is not the way I was planning on going out," said Sarah.

"If this is how it ends, so be it," Snow said. "Afraid or not I will never back down, even from a terrible beast. I say we go out fighting! We always said we would go down together— something these beasts would never understand."

"I grruunderstan," Brian managed to say.

"Did you hear that?" asked Sarah. "That was a word as sure as I am standing here."

Sarah moved closer to the bamboo poles that held her captive. Grasping one in each hand she dared to put her face right in-between them.

"Hey, get back!" ordered Snow.

"I'm telling you again. There is something about the eyes

of this one."

"Yes, they are yellow with a single black slit down the middle, just like any other beast."

"Instead of blackness I see the surface of a deep pool," she said. "And this one's eyes are not yellow. They are greenish brown."

"Trust me; the pool is as shallow as a single drop of rain."

Several beasts began pawing at Sarah through the bamboo, which interrupted her stare. She recoiled with a gasp.

"Gerraw," howled a beast in frustration.

"You're fooling yourself," said Snow. "We are a meal to him—nothing more, nothing less. If you could look into his thoughts you would see—well, even more nothing. They think nothing and understand nothing."

"They understand music," commented Ebil. He rolled on his back like a sleepy cat.

"Hey, shouldn't you be in here with us?" Snow commented. "It's your fault we got captured in the first place."

Ebil looked at him and shrugged his shoulders. "You have been brave, but I never asked to be saved."

Snow looked disgusted. "Why did we team up with you? Aren't you even going to help us find a way out of this?"

Ebil grinned. "Music may convey what words never say."

"Would you like a song?" Sarah asked Brian. She pulled a reed whistle from her vest pocket, wet her lips, and started to pipe.

"Do what you will, Sarah, but please stay back," Snow said. "The beast is evil. There is nothing to find in that thorny head."

Sarah smiled at Brian and continued to play for him.

Brian threw back his head and bellowed into the night, "Kraata! Daata!" which meant, "I am turning the humans loose."

The hoard of beasts began grumbling. Gray Beard growled loudly, and a small crowd of his irritated followers formed around him.

"I think the mutiny is underway," Brian thought.

In the next moment Brian felt something like a red-hot poker being thrust into his head. He fell to his side in agony. From where he lay, he could see a large reptilian foot next to him. He felt his scales begin to puff up for protection. Then he felt the full weight of Gray Beard land on him, causing a loud crack. The pain rippled through his bones.

Brian noticed Sarah pulling a red-tipped dart from her inside vest pocket and frantically loaded it into the whistle. With her fingers, she covered the holes on the side of the instrument and blew hard. The dart found its mark at the base of Gray Beard's neck.

"Gra!" He winced, and then yanked the bloody dart from his thick skin. He turned and focused his one-track mind on Sarah. He had the look of a quivering leopard getting ready to pounce.

Gripping his sword, Snow stepped in front of Sarah. Gray Beard swung his big arm right through the bamboo cage and backhanded him.

The entire left side of the cage collapsed, as the knight and the poles tumbled to the ground. Gerbits snorted and quickly scattered about the clearing.

During Gray Beard's distraction, Brian explored the burning pain behind his left ear. His fingers located a flaming stick jutting from his head. Grasping it tightly, he pulled it out. A spurt of green blood followed.

Gray Beard returned his attention to Brian, and Sarah followed up with another dart which struck Gray Beard in the back of his head.

Once again the beast turned his aggression toward her.

"He can't keep track of two things at once," Brian thought. Green blood dribbled down the side of Brian's neck as he sprang to his feet and jumped onto Gray Beard's back. Brian pushed the beast's head forward with a full nelson, while he pulled back on Gray Beard's arms. He could feel the cartilage ripping away from the beast's breastbone. Then he concentrated and pushed even harder.

"Grraaaa!" screamed the beast.

Brian could feel some of the fight wringing out of the monster. "The darts must have been poisoned," he thought.

"What's that crunching sound?" said Ebil, "It could be knights or ghosts or someone eating toast."

Brian began to hear a dull crunch, crunch growing out of the night. It was the sound of a thousand feet. He sniffed the air. It was ripe with the fear and salty sweat of man, and it was so thick he could actually taste it.

# CHAPTER SEVEN
# THE BATTLE

SEVERAL HUNDRED yards away, a wave of dark knights clamored over the rise. From the sound of the armor and the stomping of their feet, Brian thought there had to be at least a few thousand of them. He instinctively looked skyward and saw orange-red clouds lit by moonlight. They were low and moving toward them.

A volley of spears filled the air. As the spears found their marks, impaled beasts began to fall where they stood. Many writhed on the ground, struggling to pull the spears out of their arched bodies. Some beasts charged the knights in anger despite several impalements.

"Baarach! Montak!" yelled Brian, letting go of Gray Beard. He pointed to the opposite end of the clearing and directed the beasts to gather under the large trees.

"Grerach," said Gray Beard. Now free from Brian's grasp he refused to follow the command. He growled at Brian and scooped up a curved sickle from the ground, staggering at first. Then he ran at the knights with such speed that he cleared the distance between them—about seventy-five yards—in moments.

He cut down three knights with one full cut of the weapon. Blood sprayed everywhere as he moved into the crowd. He hacked at the torsos of the charging men as if he were harvesting wheat.

A spear impaled his chest, and it slowed him some. Then another spear and yet another pierced his flesh. He fell to one knee and was buried in a wave of spiked black armor. The massive river of swords and men trampled him into oblivion.

Brian was surprised. Even with Gray Beard's enormous strength, the black sea of charging warriors had swallowed him up in moments.

"Sarah!" yelled Snow. "As soon as we see an opening, we have got to make a break for it!"

"Sarah?" Brian thought, with sudden realization. "Hey, Cassie's mother was named Sarah. What a stroke of fate it would be, if this woman was Cassie's mom. She looks like Cassie. But Cassie said that her mother died in childbirth."

He was almost certain she had some connection to Cassie. There was something unmistakable in her smile— the curl at the corners of her mouth. Brian knelt in front of Sarah attempting to look eye to eye with her.

Sarah looked uneasy with no bamboo poles between her and the huge monster. She loaded another dart and put the reed to her lips, as she backed away.

"Get away from her!" Snow screamed, as he got back on his feet.

Brian looked toward the advancing army. "I only have a few minutes to talk her into coming with me," he thought. He moved his enlarged tongue slowly trying to force it to form words. "I knoo Cassssie."

"What?" Sarah gasped and pulled the reed from her lips. "Cassie? Did he say, 'I know Cassie'?"

"I heard, 'I am nasty'!" said the knight.

Brian concentrated and very slowly said, "Caaassssie."

"You know Cassie? Can you tell me where she is?" Sarah asked.

Brian nodded and offered Sarah his thick lumpy hand.

Sarah paused for a moment. "Okay, green one, I will come with you. But we need to hurry, and we will need fire. Fire may be the only thing that gives us a fighting chance to live until dawn."

She snatched a flaming bamboo pole from the ground and reached out to Brian. He swung her onto his back. He had a spike growing out of each hip, which made good foot pegs. She wrapped her free arm around his neck and held the torch in the other. His back was bumpy, but the bumps were smooth. Sarah could piggyback without being stabbed by his spikes.

"You're touching him!" Snow yelled, as he shook his head and came toward them with a sword in hand. "Do you want to get warts?" He ran behind them and tried to pull her off Brian's back. "Are you mad? Don't go with him, he'll kill you!"

"I've got to trust my instincts!" she yelled. "This one is different. What if he knows where my daughter is? I want you to go now and forget about me. You want me happy? Then go save yourself."

"Sarah, please listen to reason. You can no more trust a beast than you can trust a snake."

"It's something I have to do. I've got to find out what he knows about my Cassie. The last time I saw her was when I gave birth to her. Do you have any idea what it would mean to me to know anything about her?"

"I know there will be no talking you out of it. I hope this is not the last time I will ever see you. Remember our death pact? You swore on blood that we would go down together."

"Yes, of course I remember our pact. I will live to see you

again. Don't worry."

"Okay, we will do it your way. I will escape now during the madness of the battle. Follow the river down to Specters Fog and wait for me there."

"Specters Fog? That haunted swamp? Why would you want to meet there?"

"Because the knights are afraid to go in there," he answered.

"So am I," she said.

"Then we could meet at the Catacomb Caverns. It's just on the other side of the swamp."

"Catacomb Caverns—people get lost in there, too. How about picking some place that isn't creepy?"

"Look, we can't discuss this any longer. Catacomb Caverns it is. We will meet at the base of the rocky hill. And I still think he said 'nasty' not 'Cassie'…"

"Okay, okay, Catacomb Caverns," she said shaking her head. "Now stop talking and save yourself to fight another day. Go. Hurry!" She pointed to the forest. "Run into the thicket and disappear."

Brian looked back for Ebil and the little gerbit. They had already made it across the clearing and were about to vanish into the lush green undergrowth.

Brian sprang at once in the direction of the beasts congregating at the other side of the clearing. The army of knights had slowed since their initial attack. They began forming divisions at the base of the bowl-shaped clearing, as still more knights appeared over the top of the hill. Leether came striding out of the assembling knights.

"There he is," Brian thought, "Still alive and healthy, as resilient and persistent as ever. Not one bone of goodness in his entire body." Even as a beast, Brian was slightly unnerved by the mere sight of the man.

Brian continued toward the opposite side of the clearing with Sarah on his back. He wanted to gather and organize his group of wild beasts, if that was even possible. They were hungry for a fight, no question about that. He looked around at the disorganized creatures. Many had dilated pupils, and their skin was puffed up making them appear even more fearsome. Some had become so riled and aggravated that they started to fight and bite each other. The beasts were strong and fast, but they were matched up against more than a thousand knights. Only a handful of beasts had weapons at all, and those consisted of either sickles or sharpened bamboo poles.

"Grraaatah!" Brian said calling them all together. "I hope I can organize this hysteria," he thought. "I just might be able to surprise Leether with intellect. What he's counting on is a mindless charge. They can cut us all down if we run head first into rows of pointed spears."

Brian yelled again to gather the beasts. "Garrah! Garrah!" He felt his chest and arms puffing up more. His scales began to rise, as adrenalin pushed blood like a jackhammer into his chest. He looked across the clearing to the fire pit where Leether had assembled the knights.

Leether strutted back and forth, attempting to fire up the emotions of the massive army. He still had the twisted staff in one hand. Red smoke curled from its top and floated toward the red clouds that hovered above him.

Leether's voice reverberated into the night. He arched back and spoke directly to the cloud. "Justice will be done for you!" he bellowed. His eyes glowed red, and the shadowy lines in his leathery face deepened, as he snarled, "Vapor vapid, a spiritless brume. Nimbus will glow red when it takes the dead. Justice must be done!"

Brian had almost forgotten he had a rider on his back

until he felt Sarah tugging on his right ear. "If you know what I am saying, and I think you do, we can win this thing." Encouraged by her confidence, he turned his thorny head and peered into her eyes. He nodded slightly.

"Good!" she said. "You are with me. Now listen. First you have got to get the rest of your beasts into the woods. They will die if they stay in the clearing. See the red clouds forming above us right now? Backing your army of monsters into the woods will also hide your numbers."

"Exactly," Brian thought. "He won't expect us to out-think him." Brian could feel the animal side of him gaining control of his emotions as his excitement grew. It was impatient and hungry for an attack.

"Get into the woods." Brian growled in his beastly language. The beasts responded to his orders with grunts and groans. Growls echoed around them, as the monsters began to comply.

Leether waved his staff and the knights started to trot forward. The clouds swirling above them became thicker and darker.

"Brka! Brka!" Brian howled, as he motioned the beasts back into the trees.

The beasts retreated into the woods until only their front line was visible from the clearing.

"Good," said Sarah, thinking out loud. "Let's see what we have before us. The beast camp is shaped like an oblong bowl. The knights have gathered in the clearing by the fire pit. We are at the opposite end of the camp by the woods. An oval hill encircles the entire battlefield. How can we use any of it to our advantage? I know how they fight. The strength of their attack is always is in the direction they move."

"Kerrrrooosssfire," growled Brian.

"What are you saying?" asked Sarah.

"If their strength is going to come straight at us then why would we go straight at them?" Brian thought. "It is all about crossfire; it's about the angle of attack. Hit them hard from the back and sides when they have all their power focused straight ahead."

Brian waved a large circle of beasts around him and gave them instructions. He told one-third of the beasts to quietly circle around the backside of the hill to the right. The second third were told to circle around the hill to the left. Brian directed the final group to remain with him, visible at the edge of the woods, in order to draw the knights in.

The primal urge to attack continued to gnaw at him. He knew how difficult it must be for the beasts to follow his orders. But surprisingly, they did as they were told.

Brian concentrated and barked loudly, "Karta da karta."

"I am beginning to believe that you understand everything," Sarah said with a grin.

The first two platoons of beasts moved unseen through the woods, each going to its designated side of the clearing. They remained hidden by the oval hill.

Just as Brian had hoped, the army of knights moved toward him and his platoon. He stood tall with the last third of the beasts, and waited at the edge of the trees.

Sarah snickered and asked, "Who are you? You may look like a beast, but you don't act like one. I never thought I would say this to you, but good idea! Hit them from both sides."

The entire assembly of knights trotted past the fire pit. Then they picked up the pace until they were running at full stride.

Not only could Brian see the fear in the knights' eyes, he could smell it and taste it. Leether, who led the attack, advanced close enough so Brian could see him clearly. He didn't sense any fear from Leether—only a burning passion for violence and death.

"There—that's him. That's the beast over there!" Leether yelled, pointing his staff at Brian. "I want the green beast who carries the woman." Leether slowed and waved his staff forward. The warriors thundered past him like stampeding bulls.

Brian's eyes widened in surprise. He had been discovered so easily and so quickly. "Does he know I am in this beast? How could he know? Wow! He was smart enough to figure it out."

The knights were now only ten yards away.

To his platoon he said, in a low beastly growl, "Keep retreating; keep retreating." Brian backed his swarm of hungry monsters deeper into the woods.

The first of the knights entered the forest. They began cutting their way into the thick brush and trees trying to reach the seething beasts. The knights' confidence appeared to be soaring. About two hundred knights had entered the forest; a thousand or so were still in the clearing pushing forward.

"Now!" said Sarah. "Crossfire, attack, and swallow them up!"

Brian nodded his head and barked, with ear piercing volume, "KARRRAHA! KARRAHA!"

As if Brian had opened the floodgates, the beasts' pent-up energy exploded. They charged over the hill, using their powerful legs to leap halfway down it before they landed. Loud war cries bellowed from their mouths as they descended upon their startled victims. The first line of monsters wielded sharpened sickles.

The knights panicked as the beasts left a wide swath of wounded and dying warriors. Mass chaos ensued—just as Brian had planned. He thought about the story of Custer at

Little Big Horn. "The best way to beat an organized attack is with disorganization," he thought. "We are the wild savages in this battle."

Sarah whispered in Brian's ear, "Hey, my green, intelligent friend, how about we get the real evil one? Yes, Leether. Don't be afraid. You can do it. You are so strong and fast, and I will help you. We will get him together. I want him even more than you do."

The first group of knights, who had initiated the attack into the woods, slowed and looked back when they heard the cries of their comrades being slaughtered behind them. The beasts' attack was in full swing, coming from both sides. The forward thrust of Leether's attack began thinning because it couldn't make contact with a retreating enemy.

Five hundred knights had invaded the woods, and still Brian kept moving his beasts back even farther, drawing the knights in deeper and deeper. The morning sun peeked over the hill. Shafts of yellow light split between the trees, casting long shadows.

The knights were getting stretched out and weakened. It was like a rubber band being pulled to its breaking point. The first waves of knights continued forward, coming closer to Brian every second.

"KRANNA! KRANNA!" screamed Brian, telling the beasts to stand and fight. The first few knights to make contact with the beasts were tired and well out in front. The first knight to encounter Brian ran directly at him. However, he swung his sword too soon and completely missed.

Brian stepped aside and growled. Then he backhanded the warrior, lifting him off his feet. The knight flew through the air and caught his legs on a tree, which sent him spinning. The knight tumbled onto the ground and lay motionless.

Brian's tongue flickered, and hot saliva began to flow

uncontrollably from his jowls. He worked into a fit of rage as the beast within him began to gain control.

The next knight came at him with his blade raised over his head. Brian grabbed his arms and bent them back. He snatched off the knight's helmet and, without thinking, bit into the top of the man's head. Catching a momentary glimpse of the terror in the man's eyes, he stopped himself. He slowly backed his teeth out of the man's scalp and clasped both sides of his face with his huge lumpy fingers. The man was in shock—unable to speak, unable to breath. He trembled as he awaited his certain death.

"Ruun!" Brian yelled, and he shoved the knight backward. "Ruun or diiie!"

The knight fell back, caught his balance, and ran headlong into another beast that pounced on top of him.

Brian knelt down and clutched his scaly face. "What am I?" he thought, "I almost bit off that guy's head. I can't lose control like that again."

"You are a very special beast," Sarah said softly. "You were talking! I heard you say. 'Run or die.' You have compassion."

But the other beasts showed no mercy. The knights were being slaughtered. They had been thinned out sufficiently that the beasts had time to destroy everything that came at them. A few beasts had been injured or destroyed, but hundreds of crumpled knights blanketed the forest floor.

Suddenly, in succession, two loud cracks of thunder echoed across the clearing. The knights froze. Then they turned and began to retreat from the woods as fast as their stubby legs would carry them.

"That thunder clap was probably a signal from Leether," said Sarah. "Leether is obsessed, but in no way is he stupid. He is adjusting to our trickery by getting his troops out of the woods. Then he'll reinforce against our attack in the clearing. No doubt he is in some kind of disbelief that we outwitted him." Suddenly, with a look of shock on her face, she yelled, "Oh, no! Look above you!"

"Grah?"

"The red curtain of death!"

Distracted during the melee, they had not noticed the red cloud settling over the tops of the trees. Now they could see Leether's plan, but it was too late. He had pulled the knights out of the woods so he could lower the red cloud into the forest. Red-orange, gelatinous globs oozed down the branches. The cloud was so massive that it blocked the morning sun.

"It's too large to escape it," said Sarah. "There will be some knights that don't make it out of the forest in time either, but that won't bother Leether. Fire is the only defense against the cloud."

She shrieked as the goo closed around the tops of the tree. "If I can get a good fire going we may have a chance. Over there," she said, pointing at a massive half-dead tree. Some of its leaves had been baked dry by the sun.

Brian dug in his toes and in two springing steps had her directly under the branches. Sarah quickly began setting the low lying leaves and branches on fire. The tree caught immediately and became engulfed in crackling flames. Burning embers rained down on them, but they couldn't move away from the trunk because the fire protected them from the cloud goo. Sarah crouched in a ball and pulled her scaled coat over the top of her head. The cloud continued its descent, and as it did, a small opening formed around the burning branches.

The goo circled them and covered the rest of the forest. It was unnerving to have it pass so close. Then the cloud began to settle on the forest floor. The ground and forest animals were coated in the sticky gelatinous blob. As the cloud came down, the pool of goo grew deeper and deeper.

Growling beasts tried to claw their way through it but the goo clung to them, stretching but not breaking; numbing them and wearing them down. The great strength and power of the beasts appeared useless against such an enemy. The cloud began to bubble as it combined with the soil, and the beasts sank into it.

Then the goo on the ground closed in tighter around the base of the burning tree. "Tentacles will cooooome," said Brian.

"Right. The tentacles will reach out of the slime. We have got to get out of here. The cloud can't be beaten. The only way is up," said Sarah "Think you can get us up this tree without getting burned?"

The leaves had burned up in a flash, and now the tree was mostly smoldering branches and glowing red bark. He put his scaly hand on the side of the tree and pressed his palm into the steaming sap. He felt the hot bark singe his thick palms, but it was a dull pain. He looked back at her and nodded.

Brian sprang and dug his claws deep into its trunk. The red-hot embers scorched his hands and chest but the pain remained distant. He grunted and pushed his huge body upward along the trunk. The tree creaked as it strained to hold his enormous weight.

"Keep going," Sarah yelled. "My coat is shielding me from the embers. My ankles are getting burned, but I think I can hold on."

As Brian climbed, he heard his beasts growling as they fought with their last gurgling breaths. On a charred branch near the top of the tree, he paused for a moment. He saw that the entire cloud was completely below them. Dark tentacles were now rising out of the goo, pulling in the last few surviving beasts. The forest floor, once covered with brush and leaves, was a burbling swamp of reddish muck. Tentacles slithered blindly reaching out to find something to pull into the slime.

All was lost. The beasts in the forest had all but disappeared into the ooze. Brian's vantage point also gave him a good view of the clearing. About thirty beasts were still battling in the open but any chance for victory had slipped away. The knights had regrouped and were holding their own.

Many of the beasts were starting to run off into the woods to save themselves. He had hopes that Ebil and the little gerbit had escaped into the forest during the battle. It felt serene to be sitting high atop a smoking tree with all the chaos and death so far below.

Now that the last of the beasts had been swallowed up, the goo began to vaporize. Red smoke rose rapidly off the forest floor and began to reform into a growing red cloud above them.

Still, the skirmish in the clearing continued. Brian was surprised at how many beasts refused to escape with their lives. They chose to stay and fight when death was certain. Maybe they stayed just for the pleasure of a good fight. Despite being victorious, the knights had taken heavy casualties—only a few hundred still stood.

Just then Brian noticed a circular pool of goo that had remained on the ground. It was forming a moat around the very tree they were hiding in. Brian tried to talk without using the lower part of his throat, where the growls came from. Moving his thick tongue carefully, he spoke clearly for the first time. "He knows."

"What? What does he know?" asked Sarah. "You mean he knows we are here? Hey, you were talking!"

Brian pointed at the base of the tree. Thick tentacles grew out of the circle of goo and slithered up the trunk. They were momentarily held back by the last few burning embers at the base of the tree.

"It is just a matter of time before the tree is consumed by them," she said.

Several loud thunderclaps sounded overhead, and lightning splattered across the sky. Then the cloud opened up with a drenching rain.

"After the cloud eats, it always rains so hard you can scarcely see. The flames will be put out. We're painted into a corner," said Sarah, as gray smoke rose from the tree. She looked below and saw the tentacles snaking toward them. "We can't climb down."

The gooey appendages wrapped themselves around the tree and squeezed it.

Sarah frowned. "I have seen tentacles many times. There is no end to how far they can stretch. It's like unraveling a thread on a sweater. How far out can you jump?" she asked.

Brian calculated the width of the circle of goo at the tree's base. "Not far enough," he said.

"In other words, we are toast," she said. The stress began to show in the quivering corners of Sarah's mouth. "Think! That's what my mother would always say. While others freeze you think. Block everything else out. Okay, what do I have to work with? I have a beast and a big tree. We need to get about twenty yards beyond the trunk of the tree to clear the moat of goo. We have maybe thirty seconds before those wormy tentacles reach us."

Turning her attention to Brian, she said, "Do you think you could you tip this tree over so that we could ride it down?"

"Like a pole-vaulter?" Brian said.

"Not exactly, but something like it. Wobble the tree so it

96

breaks off at the base." Then she cocked her head to one side and said, "Hey! How do you even know the term pole vault? That's a word from my past life."

Ignoring her question, Brian concentrated on his words. "Haaaang on," he said as a tentacle reached Brian's foot and inched up to his calf.

He began to rock the tree.

Sarah dropped the torch and hung on for her life in the slippery, pelting rain. She pulled in tighter with both arms and hugged Brian's thick beastly neck. "Who are you?" she whispered, "Who is in there? You are no hell beast. You're a guardian angel."

Brian's rocking began to gain momentum, the tree swaying back and forth until it began to make contact with the trees on either side. He was amazed at the distance the old tree could travel without breaking. The tree creaked and groaned but did not snap. Brian strained and shifted his weight, all the while trying to shake a stubborn tentacle from his foot. It seemed at any moment the top of the tree would sway all the way down and touch the ground, yet it did not break.

Then suddenly…CRA-A-CK!

In the next instant the tree careened toward the dirt. And then it fell, pummeling through branches and smaller trees. Moments before the tree made contact with the ground, Brian executed a high, long leap. He landed with such force that his large feet dented the soil. A shower of burnt leaves and twigs followed as the tree hit.

"We're clear!" Sarah shouted.

She still clung to Brian, as leaves showered over them. She shoved her fist into the air, and shouted, "YAY! AWOOOOO! We're still here! You did it! The tree cleared the moat."

Brian did an instinctive funny dance, while spinning in a circle. It resembled an Irish jig combined with a seizure.

"Okay, now focus," she said. "It won't be long before the goo or cloud or whatever will be on us again. Leether's not going to give up. So, my green, lumpy, bumpy buddy, it's time to move!"

Brian took a large springy first step. He felt Sarah's grip tighten as she pressed her head into his neck.

Sarah laughed. "I would love to wallow for a moment in Leether's disappointment. But we'd better keep moving."

Brian sent small trees toppling out of the way as he cut a destructive path through the woods.

"Keep running hard and long," Sarah said. "We need to put some time between us and them."

Lighting shattered the dark morning sky, and Brian used the spurts of light to navigate the eerie surroundings. Once again, the clouds broke open with full force, and an angry rain riddled them like bullets.

# CHAPTER EIGHT
# LUMPY AND SMELLINDA

"WE ARE Leether's new obsession," yelled Sarah, as the wind and rain whipped her long coat.

Brian figured she didn't really know how much he understood because she kept rambling on—much like someone would talk to a favorite pet. "Obsession is a trait of the tirelessly insane. I don't know what you did to him in the past, but it must have been really good, and now you've outsmarted him! Ha! Think of it. How fabulous! Outsmarted by a beast of despair! Well, you certainly have his attention now, don't you? But as much as I am enjoying the moment, I do realize we are in very deep. Now he will hunt us as long as we breathe."

The thunder rumbled farther behind them. The cloud, now dark red and with a full belly, had completely risen from the forest. Dawn had lifted the veil of darkness around them.

Brian moved like a wrecking ball through the trees. Now that he was well clear of the hovering red clouds, he took a few more bounding steps and then came to an abrupt stop.

Sarah jumped to the ground and stretched. She bent her arms over her head and took a long look at her ugly new friend as he pulled enormous amounts of air into his lungs. "If you truly understand me, please tell me what you know about my daughter before something else happens."

"She thinks yourrr dead."

"Cassie thinks I'm dead?" Sarah shook her head in disgust. "That sounds like the truth. Leether would want to make sure she never came looking for me. Years ago, Snow, Skhat, and I all tried to stop the crazy cloud worship and human sacrifices Leether was instigating. That's why Leether had us banished—sent over the mountain. So now, tell me quickly, Mr. Beast, what do you know about my Cassie?"

"She's aaamazing!"

Sarah's smile could not have grown any larger. "What is Cassie to you?"

"Guurl friend."

"Girl friend?" Sarah said with disdain. She gathered herself, as if she had suddenly realized that she might have insulted the large beast. "Please don't take this wrong, but a mother has hopes her daughter might end up with someone …well, less lumpy. You are a fine beast…um, actually the best I've ever seen. But you must understand there are biological problems—like grandchildren, for instance. I mean what would they look like?"

"Grrrrandchildren?"

"No, I am sorry, I know everyone has a somewhat distorted self-image, but when I look at you, I see a monster. You are smart; I'll give you that. And the talking? Well, it blows me away."

Brian concentrated and answered slowly. He had been working very hard to learn the right way to move his thick tongue and keep the growl out of the bottom of his throat. He painstakingly told Sarah how he was human when he visited this world once before and met up with Cassie. He explained how his aura came to be locked inside the beast after Leether had captured it in a glassy ball. There were a few growls in his speech but she seemed to understand every bit of it.

"That is a wild and impressive story, but how do I know it's the truth?"

"I fooound a doll in the tunnel. Was it yours?"

Sarah's face contorted. "You found my porcelain doll? I must have dropped it there twenty some years ago. That's right, I remember that day well. I was playing with it by the pond. I set in on a toy boat and waded in, and then the pond took me down."

Brian dropped his head and gently put his heavy hand on her shoulder. "Cassie is safe at home with your mother."

"My mother!"

Brian nodded.

Sarah raised an eyebrow. "What is my mother's name?"

"Rae…gerrr name is Rae."

Sarah's face reddened, and then like a pot coming to a boil, tears spilled down her face. "Okay, now you got me."

Sarah was silent for a long moment. She rubbed the tears with the side of her hand. A chirping bird filled the silence as Sarah regained her composure.

Then Brian began to describe Cassie in glowing terms. As he talked, Sarah stared up at him, not as someone who looks at a thorny beast, but as someone looks at a reliable friend.

"Will you help me?" she asked.

"If I can," Brian answered.

"Can you safely get me to Catacomb Caverns? That's where I am supposed to meet up with Snow. I know he must be very worried about me."

Brian nodded his big thorny head.

"He was so mad that I didn't go with him. It feels odd being separated from my two banished knights. They were like family. I can still hardly accept that Skhat was killed in the blink of an...." She stopped in mid-sentence and listened.

Brian's sensitive ears perked up. He heard a sound like runaway boulders smashing through the forest behind him. He leaped in the air and spun around to face the disruption. Landing solidly, he took a wide stance, extended his claws, and stood ready to take on whatever was going to erupt from the thick cluster of trees.

Sarah grabbed a spike on his shoulder and swung herself onto his back. First, there was the scurry of small animals and birds taking flight. Then the trees began to shake, sending leaves floating to the ground. Suddenly, two beasts exploded through the trees running at top speed. When they saw Brian, they leaped into the air and danced around with excitement, while fragments of tree branches rained down. They embraced Brian with big beastly hugs, and Sarah, still on Brian's back, got bumped and crushed between the sweaty monsters.

"Get them off me!" Sarah yelled.

"Graflua!" Brian barked. The beasts released their embrace and tried to contain their exuberance.

"They must have followed us," said Sarah. "Any beasts that survived the battle are probably scattered all over the forest."

"They must have trrr-acked us using their amazing noses," Brian said, touching his moist snoot with his finger.

Sarah laughed. "I think they might have also followed the path of destruction you left behind." She pointed back through the swath of broken and toppled trees.

One of the two beasts had a spear imbedded in his left shoulder and a bloody green diagonal cut across his chest.

The scales had opened up showing the pulsating muscles beneath. The other beast had a glob of red cloud goo still clinging onto its shoulder like a leach.

"They're coming with us," said Brian. "We're much stronger with them."

"Are you sure about that? They'll kill me just for sport, like a cat does with a mouse."

"They will do what I say—I think."

The beast with the open wound was struggling to tilt his head so he could lick his own blood, which ran freely. Brian grabbed onto the spear that jutted from his shoulder, and tugged. The beast squirmed awkwardly.

The spear would not budge. Realizing the solution, Brian broke off the barbed tip, which stuck out the beast's back, and then gripped the spear tightly from the front, "Hold still, Lumpy," Brian barked. He braced his foot against the beast's chest and, with a huge yank, pulled the spear free.

The beast howled, and dark green blood squirted, at first, and then ran down his scales and legs, pooling on the ground.

"What do I do now?" said Brian.

Sarah slipped off his back and picked up a smooth round stone about the size of the wound. "Here," she said, brushing the dirt off from it, "try this."

Brian took the stone and pushed it part way into the bloody hole. He balled up his fist and thumped it solidly for good measure. The beast recoiled a little, and then looked at Brian, rather pleased with his doctoring.

"Will that stone really work to control the bleeding?" Brian asked.

Sarah shrugged, "Who knows? Who cares? Just remember," she said, as she climbed onto his back, "Mr. Lumpy and Ms. Smelly here are animals. Just as a pet snake is still a snake, a friendly beast is still a beast. They are not like you. Just look at their cold, serpent-like eyes."

"Just stick close to me and you'll be fine."

"That was a complete sentence! You are talking so much better— you almost have the hang of it. And fine, they can come with us. We can call the boy Lumpy, and the girl, um, something more feminine than Smelly."

"How about Smell—inda?" Brian laughed with a gruff, "Gra-ha-ha-ha."

"Okay, Lumpy and Smellinda." Sarah smiled.

Brian looked to the sky and saw the red cloud was gaining ground again. "Let's keep moving," he said.

He grunted at the other beasts and leapt forward. In the next moment they were all crashing through the forest together.

"You run so fast that everything looks like a blur," Sarah said. She ducked her head behind Brian's powerful shoulders to avoid the snapping branches. "Cut to the right," she yelled. "We'll take a detour and float downstream to throw Leether off track."

Brian made the turn and then sped on at a steady pace. With the two beasts following close behind, they ran until early afternoon. Brian guessed that Sarah was taking a thrashing, and he marveled that she didn't complain.

Thunder echoed in the distance, and after a time it sounded more like a low rumble. Brian felt great relief when he could no longer see any red clouds in the sky.

He sprang over a jagged incline and cleared the crest of a hill. As he descended toward the bottom, he stopped and twitched his ear. "I hear water pushing against the rocks." He sniffed the air. "Fish—I smell fish. Food and water are on the other side of the next hill."

"Water?" asked Sarah.

He forced the corners of his mouth up into a beastly

smile. "Lunch."

Lunging forward, he scrambled up the next rise. From the summit, he peered through the trees and caught sight of a small river cutting through the sun-streaked forest below.

Lumpy and Smellinda raced past them and crashed into the shallow river, sending turtles and frogs scrambling. Brian could see the sun sliding along the rippling current. Even from his spot at the top of the hill, he could see smooth powder-blue stones resting on the riverbed. He followed the beasts down the hill and flopped headlong into the clear, cool stream.

Sarah tumbled over his head into the water, which was only up to her waist. She staggered to her feet in the strong current, and emerged soaking wet. "Hey! Let me know before you put on the brakes," she said, as she flipped back her hair.

Brian gulped fresh water, his head completely submerged. The other two beasts splashed and dove like hungry bears. They caught frogs and fish and, for the most part, swallowed them whole.

Brian raised his head out of the water in time to see Sarah swimming back to shore. "What are you doing?" he asked, as he shook water out of his ears like a dog.

"It's a little dangerous being in the river with two thrashing food-frenzied beasts. Besides, I want it to look like we followed the river upstream toward the sunny, inviting hills," she said, as she picked an apple from an overhanging branch. "But, in fact, we will go downstream toward the ghostly swamp called Specters Fog."

Brian smiled. "Clever woman," he thought. He sat in the water and watched her imprint her feet in the river's muddy bank. After a time, she returned and slipped into the water—a safe distance from the two beasts.

Brian crunched on a whole fish. He was amazed by

the flavor and satisfaction he got from the meat. He knew under normal circumstances he would find raw meat quite disgusting.

With his belly full, he climbed back onto the riverbank and basked in the warm sun. He watched as the two beasts wrestled and splashed in the water. They seemed to be having a good time. Then he observed Sarah eating her apple and disturbing the small stones upstream with her toes.

It actually felt kind of homey, like some kind of demented family picnic. It was the first relaxing moment Brian had experienced in days. A gentle breeze tickled the leaves, and dots of light danced off the sparkling water as it bubbled smoothly over the rocks. Brian was tired, and this place had him entranced. His eyelids gave in to the peace of the moment and began to slowly close.

A high-pitched scream shattered the stillness. Playtime had gotten a little rough with the two beasts and it had, naturally, escalated into a fight to the death. Lumpy, the wounded beast, weakened by his blood loss, was getting the worst of it. Smellinda was expressionless as she held her playmate under the water. What chilled Brian the most was that the beast could kill without any forethought or remorse whatsoever.

"Stop it!" Brian yelled. The beast looked up blankly. "I mean, kearata!"

Smellinda released her victim. Her ears drooped, as if she were a bad dog. Lumpy's body rose slowly to the surface, attached to a thin ribbon of dark green blood flowing from his chest wound.

"I can't believe how cold-hearted they are," Brian said.

"They have no soul," said Sarah. "They are hollow shells that eat to live and live to eat. Think of them as simple predators, not necessarily evil. They're just doing what they were designed to do."

"And they are designed to do evil," said Brian "Trust me, I should know. I have felt it burning inside me. They don't just live to eat. They take pleasure from suffering and death. If that is not a definition of evil, what is?"

"Well…you would know. Why do I make excuses for them? I have an idea. Why don't you walk upstream a ways and bring the dead beast with you."

Sliding back into the water Brian gently took the beastly body out of Smellinda's hands. She avoided eye contact with Brian, and tucked her tail between her legs.

"Come here, Lumpy," said Brian as he pulled the floating dead beast by the arm. He hoisted Lumpy's limp carcass onto his shoulder.

"Break off a few of the low branches, too," Sarah called out. "They will see the blood trail and go upstream. Meanwhile, we'll be floating downstream."

Brian nodded. "More misdirection, good thinking."

About fifty yards upstream Brian found a partially submerged tree. It had been upended, and several broken roots stuck up like spikes. Brian lifted the dead weight of the lumpy beast and slammed it down hard, impaling it on the fallen tree trunk. "This should make Lumpy stay put and provide a nice blood trail for Leether to follow."

Brian stretched out his arms, lay back in the water, and sucked in a lung full of air. Becoming quite buoyant, he let the current carry him.

Sarah pushed herself into deeper water. Smellinda sat in the shallows, content to pull up grass from the bottom and eat the roots.

Brian suddenly realized that if Smellinda decided to attack Sarah, he would never get there in time. "I hope Sarah knows that she is safest when the beast is distracted. If

Smellinda looks her way, she might decide to do what beasts are designed to do."

The closer Brian drifted toward Sarah, the better he felt. He could see Sarah's head as he bobbed with the rippling current. He gave her a silly wave.

She waded farther into the stream and held onto his stomach and chest as he floated by. She rested her head against his shoulder, and the smooth current carried them. Without a sound, Smellinda pulled the wad of river grass from her jaws and lunged forward to follow them into the deeper part of the stream.

After a while, the stream widened into a river, and the current quickened. Brian relaxed and soaked in the relative peace and quiet for several hours.

• • •

"We're getting close to that swamp called Specters Fog," Sarah said, startling Brian from his daydreaming. "Catacomb Caverns will be just on the other side of it."

"How can you tell that we're near the swamp?" asked Brian. "There aren't any obvious landmarks."

"The smell—it's a swampy, stale, boggy moor kind of smell."

"I wondered what that smell was," he said, lowering his legs until his feet touched the river bottom.

Sarah slid away from Brian and waited for him to kneel. Then she positioned herself on his back. He stood slowly and walked ashore. He put his hands on his hips and scanned the woods.

Smellinda stood alongside him. After several attempts to position her hands in the correct position, she managed to stand exactly as Brian stood.

Sarah laughed. "Smellinda admires you."

The sun sent long shadows stretching through the woods. It was nearing the end of a long day. Sniffing the air, Brian cut between the trees. Sarah rode high on his back, and Smellinda bounded a few steps behind, like a new puppy.

Sarah pushed herself up higher on Brian's massive shoulders to gain a better vantage point. As they reached the top of a small grassy hill, Specters Fog came into view in the lowlands before them. It was a large area of swamp and marsh about five miles wide. A white mist clung to the surface, while black gnarled tree branches poked through the white mist here and there, like the arms of a snowman. The darkened tree roots rose out of the bog. Small patches of soil clung to them like thousands of tiny islands just big enough to sit on.

"Why do they call this swamp Specters Fog, and why won't the knights go in there?" Brian asked as he descended the hill.

Sarah leaned forward and spoke with her mouth next to his ear. "They say that Specters Fog is tangled with ghosts thick as weeds. They crawl, barely seen—like a spider's shadow in the mist."

"What is that supposed to mean? Are they actual ghosts?"

"That's how the old story goes. Ghosts or not, it is of no consequence. All I know for sure is this: There is something awful in there. They say what goes in never comes out. We are not going in there. We can get to Catacomb Caverns to meet up with Snow by simply walking around it."

Brian stopped just outside the rim of black trees and shallow marsh. Sarah climbed down and rubbed the soreness out of her shoulders. Smellinda dove in the muck with a loud splash. She came up dripping with mud, a salamander squirming in her mouth.

A raindrop hit Sarah on the head, and another splattered onto her arm. She glanced at her hand and then looked up. "Skrud! Nimbus has been tracking us! We didn't fool anyone."

A large shadow spread across the hill and over the wet lowland grasses. Above them, the massive red cloud pushed through the air.

"We're exposed out here in the clearing," yelled Brian. "Quick! Into the swamp! We'll hide in the mist."

# CHAPTER NINE
# SPECTERS FOG

Brian scooped up Sarah before she could speak and tucked her under his big scaly arm. He charged headlong into the dangerous bog with Smellinda close behind. The ground became less stable as it squished under his feet. First it was muddy, and then more water than dirt. But he didn't slow his pace until he was certain they were well into the swamp.

Neither Brian nor Sarah spoke as they crept toward what could be their demise. Brian's muscles tensed, ready for something—anything—to leap out at them. As they inched along, the cool white vapor crept toward them out of the middle of the bog.

"I'm not sure this will work, but there's no point in turning back now," Sarah whispered. "As long as we are in, we might as well cut right through the middle of the swamp. It's the shortest distance to the caverns."

Brian helped Sarah climb onto his back. "Something's out there," he murmured.

Spanish moss hung from bare branches and swayed gently in the lazy breeze. Brian ducked behind a tree. He reached out and grabbed Smellinda by the arm and pulled her behind the trunk with him. Squinting, he scanned the area for any movement.

He saw mist swirl out of the haze. Then the gelatinous red ooze snaked through the trees, like a giant floating worm, as it followed their trail.

"The mist won't conceal us," Sarah said in a hushed tone. "The cloud doesn't have eyes. It uses its sense of smell."

"It's sniffing for us?"

"Let's get underwater!"

"Take a deep breath," said Brian. He pushed Smellinda's head under as he took himself and Sarah down into the swampy water just before the cloud came around the tree. Sarah held out for several minutes. Brian sensed her throat beginning to involuntarily restrict and contract, but she held fast to his neck and stayed under. Eventually he knew she couldn't last one more moment. He surfaced and sucked in a cool breath of misty air. To his relief, he saw that the cloud had moved on.

Brian tried to peer through the haze. "This mist is so thick I can actually taste it. My mom always called fog like this pea soup. I would rather eat ten bowls of that crap right now instead of tasting this swamp."

"You taste it?"

"Yeah, I can't turn these monster taste buds off. I also can't turn off my eyes or ears. I am so dialed-in to this place it is ridiculous. Wait," said Brian. He opened his eyes wide and concentrated, but still he could not see through the fog. "Something else is out there. I can't see it but I can feel the vibrating thump of its heart."

Sarah waved her hand to clear the mist but it only swirled in front of her. "Is it Snow?"

"No, I don't think it's him. Hey! Now I'm hearing more

heartbeats."

"How many?"

"Answering that would be like trying to count cricket chirps on a summer night. Let's just say there are lots and lots of them."

"Specters?"

"Maybe. I can't see them—that's for sure. But where I come from ghosts don't have beating hearts."

"The knights won't come in here because the scary stories are real. The truth is, we might actually be safer with Leether than staying in the swamp."

Brian dug his claws into the dirt and pulled his large frame onto some grass that clung to the roots of a black tree. Sarah climbed down and stood next to Smellinda, who scooted her back against the trunk.

"The cloud will come back, and we can't stay underwater forever," said Brian.

"We need to mask our scent. I noticed that your ugly girlfriend here still has a glob of cloud goo on her left shoulder. When part of the cloud is cut away, it takes a day before it becomes its own organism. We should boil it."

"Why?"

"There are only two things that can kill the cloud: heat and basil. Basil doesn't grow in the swamp but I can make fire. We can boil the goo to kill it and then rub it on ourselves. Like most things, the cloud can't smell its own stink. If the cloud can't smell us then it can't find us."

Sarah knelt between Brian and Smellinda. She took a small curved knife from her vest pocket and leaned in carefully to scrape the red blob from Smellinda's shoulder.

The beast snapped, and in a flash had Sarah pinned to the tree by her throat.

"She's breaking my neck!" Sarah squawked.

"Grrahh!" Brian growled, as he swung his big arm over Sarah's head and jabbed his claws into Smellinda's face.

The beast jerked back and let go. Her eyes dropped in submission.

Sarah rubbed her sore neck. "Just relax!" she yelled at Smellinda.

The beast's eyes followed Sarah's every move, but her body remained still.

Brian lifted the red blob off Smellinda's shoulder with his clawed fingers and flipped it upside down in his palm. He squeezed it firmly. Dark red tentacles began to protrude. "It reminds me of a jellyfish."

"The best way to defeat your enemies is to first learn all you can about them," Sarah said.

Brian felt his palm becoming numb. He jiggled the blob for a moment. It rose up on one end. "We should heat this right away."

Sarah poked at the blob in his palm. "See how it's all red? It's gorged with blood." She balled up a piece of moss and made a tee pee of sticks over the top of it. She then took a piece of flint and a metal cup out of her pocket. Expertly she lit a small ember and proceeded to coax it into a flame by blowing at the base with little puffs of air.

Once the flame took on a life of its own, Sarah had Brian put the blob into the cup. She held the cup with a stick through the handle over the fire until it gave off an awful gray smoke that choked her. She turned her head away so she could breathe the good air as the smoke drifted past her. The goo quickly began to bubble and pop like hot pudding. She dipped her finger in and tasted the thick brew.

"Yuck! That's terrible! But tasting is the only way to know it's done, which it is. Now it won't numb you anymore." She first spread some on her arm, and then she began to rub the jellylike blend on her face and even in her hair. "Go ahead and take some," she said.

Brian dipped his lumpy fingers into the concoction and rubbed it between his hands. He smeared it on his face and arms. He laughed. "And I thought I was stinky before."

"Nothing stinks like the scent of the red cloud," she said as Brian continued rubbing the hot goo over his scales. He realized they had been completely ignoring the third member of their group. Smellinda was quietly starring into the foggy abyss of the marsh. Brian reached past Sarah, in an attempt to rub the mixture onto Smellinda's shoulder. The beast shoved Brian's hand away and growled.

"We smell like the cloud," Sarah said. "She doesn't want to have anything to do with this stuff."

Smellinda wrinkled her nose and sneezed. She winced and blinked, and then scooted farther away from Brian. For the first time, she looked at him with disdain.

Sarah surveyed their surroundings. "It will be black as pitch soon. It would be best if we don't spend the night here. If we can keep moving, we can get to the other side. No doubt there will be various nasty creatures racing to check us out—spiders, snakes, bats, flies and, of course, the specters. I don't even want to think about them. Hopefully they'll get one whiff of us and keep moving. I would love to get out of here before dark."

Brian nodded and slipped back into the water, sinking up to his chest. He leaned against the dirt mound so that Sarah could climb onto his back. Smellinda plunged head first into the marsh and emerged chomping on a mouth full of black roots.

"How much do you know about the cloud? How does Leether control it?" Brian asked, as he worked his feet forward through the misty bog.

"Basically, this is what I know: The cloud lives inside Leether's body. They share thoughts, emotions, and purpose. They are one and the same. And the best way to explain how the cloud works is to compare it to water, which consists of three forms—liquid, gas, and solid. The cloud also has three forms. When it goes into the ground, it combines with the soil and you get muck. The muck solidifies and creates tentacles. In its vapor form, it is a red mist. Under normal conditions it's a blobby cloud, and can deliver rain and lightning, just like real clouds do."

"Why does it always rain after it eats?"

"That is the final part of the digestion process. It must expel the water that has been replaced by blood. The more it eats the harder it will rain. When the cloud is dark red, it has just eaten."

Brian opened his mouth to ask another question, but was interrupted by an eerie voice echoing from the deepest bowels of the bog. It was melodic, in a very disturbing sort of way. "We will take youoooo" it sang quietly.

"Did you hear that?" Brian froze, listening intently.

"Time to dieeee?"

"There it is again," whispered Sarah. "The specters are singing to us. It's just like the myth. They serenade you before..."

"Before what?"

"Before they take you."

Then the voice sang out through the mist again, only this time louder and more forceful. "Time to dieee?"

"Wow," said Brian. "That was creepy. It sounded less like a question and more like a statement. Well, if the specters want to take me out, I'm going to take as many of them with me as I can, and the way I feel right now that will be a whole lot of them."

Brian began to puff up, and his scales started to rise. The slits in his greenish brown eyes grew round and black. "Grrrrraaaahh!"

"Keep control of that monster inside you. You can't even see the specters so how are you going to fight them? You can't charge in and take on the whole swamp with no plan."

Brian nodded, and his scales started to lie back down.

It became quiet and still again. They continued to cautiously move forward through the haze. The darker it got, the bolder the seemingly timid creatures of the marsh became. They wailed, chirped, and croaked—all blending into a noisy racket. No beautiful sunset here. The last drop of light faded as the fog encased them.

Smellinda tagged along a short distance behind. She was entertaining herself by thumping turtles on their backs and diving in after frogs.

Through a momentary break in the mist, Brian saw that they were nearing the outer rim of the swamp. He heard distant voices and caught a glimpse of yellow flickers of fire just beyond the bog. He peered between the broken branches of a rotten log that rested in the marsh. As the mist cleared again, he could make out Black Knights setting up tents and equipment. Next to a large blistering fire sat Leether, directing a work crew.

"How did Leether beat us here?" said Sarah. "He stays one step ahead of us. He must have gone straight to Catacomb Caverns, while we were floating downstream. We're safe from him as long as we stay in the swamp. Problem is, Snow can't meet us at the caverns because Leether is setting up right in front of them. Incredible!"

Leether turned his head toward them and seemed to be scanning the swamp.

"I don't think he can see us," said Brian.

Sarah wiped the murky water from her eyes. "I hate to say this, but we'd better spend the night in the swamp. Then in the morning we can sneak up for a closer look. I want to know what Leether is up to. It's too much of a coincidence that he's setting up camp at the very spot we were going to meet Snow. Let's find a dry spot and brace ourselves for who knows what might come out of the swamp. No fire tonight. I don't want Leether to know we're in here."

Brian pulled himself onto a small grassy island. Sarah climbed down and worked the kinks out of her neck. He scratched behind his ear with one sharp claw and rested against a tree. Smellinda already had dug in and was curling up like a fat cat. The moonlight could not penetrate the misty swamp. But it gave off just enough light to give the bog an eerie yellow glow.

Brian peered through the mist and tracked the movement all around them. "If I had human eyes, I wouldn't see anything," he thought. "There are thousands of creatures in this swamp, and I'm the biggest and scariest of them all. I'm not going to tell Sarah what's going on out there. It would only keep her from getting rest." He took a big beastly breath and rested his thorny head against the tree. He had no idea what kind of day tomorrow would bring.

The beast within him had retreated into the deep shadows of his subconscious. It had not interrupted his thoughts for most of the day. It was discomforting; he knew that losing his guard, even for a moment, could give the beast a chance to take control and do something horrible.

It had occurred to Brian that he and Sarah should sleep in shifts, with someone always awake. But they were both so exhausted. Who was going to stay awake? He finally convinced himself they should both rest. He was confident that he would awaken at the first sound of danger. With that in mind, Brian relaxed his shoulders and back, closed his eyes, and succumbed to sleep.

. . .

He slipped into a deep slumber, which soon led to dreams of being back on the farm. He was in his old bed, and the sheets were light and soft. He could smell the fresh cool air; the morning sun was shining through the window.

He tried to lift his arms but he could not. He concentrated hard and commanded his body to move, but he remained motionless—not a twitch, shiver, or shake. He couldn't even raise a single goose bump. It was as if he were cut out of stone.

His eyes were fixed on the spinning ceiling fan, and he couldn't blink. He didn't breathe; his heart was still.

He heard a soft noise, very quiet at first. Someone was crying. The person came into view, and it was Cassie. Her head rested on his shoulder, as she held his hand.

She lifted her head, and Brian saw that her beautiful face was red and contorted. Tears flowed down her freckled cheeks.

"Wake up!" she burst, in a sudden rage. She shook him and yelled again, angrier. "Wake up!" She smacked his chest with her open hand.

Mom and Tommy moved into the doorway. Mom shook her head. "You must accept it, sweetheart. We must all accept it and be strong. He's not coming back. My heart is broken, too; part of me has died with him."

"You promised, Brian," Cassie cried. "You promised you'd come back! You said you would be back by breakfast! That was a week ago." She began to weep uncontrollably. "Come back to me!"

Mom placed a gentle hand on Cassie's back. "He is gone. If he could have come back to us you know he would have. We have lost him."

Then Brian's vision became hazy, and he heard their preacher's voice: "Blessed are the pure in heart for they shall see God. Blessed are the peacemakers for they shall be called the children of God." He touched Brian's forehead and, in a closing gesture, pulled the sheet over Brian's head.

Brian wanted to call out, but he couldn't force even a whisper to escape his lips. He was frozen in time. Muffled voices echoed in his head. He screamed as hard as he could, but no air pushed between his dry lips.

Brian's soundless scream shocked him into consciousness. He jerked forward and gasped for breath. "Oh my gosh, what was that?"

He blinked, feeling somewhat bewildered. He found that he was waist-deep somewhere in the dark black bog. "I must have been sleepwalking and ended up way out here. Wow, what a nightmare! That was on a whole new level. Could my real body be dying? How long will they wait before they bury me?"

He tried to get his bearings, "Where the heck am I? Where is Sarah?" He glanced around. Leether's campfire appeared as a small glowing speck of light way off in the distance.

He heard a growl and realized Smellinda had been standing silently with her back to him the entire time. There was a strange taste in his mouth, and then he recognized it as fresh blood.

He realized that the beast within him had taken complete control while he was lost in sleep. "Apparently I have been terrorizing the swamp with Smellinda," he thought. He knew they were in the black belly of the bog and had been or were about to be fighting something. His chest was puffed out and his scales stood out like millions of tiny shields.

It was strangely quiet and still. The air was filled with tension, like the moment before a coiled snake strikes.

He saw fractured movements in the darkness to the side and then in front of him. Creatures of some kind were closing around them. Out of the corner of his eye he spotted Smellinda, and she was smiling. "She lives for this," he thought. "My guess is that we're taking on the specters in their own backyard and she couldn't be happier. How did I sleep through all this?"

He heard a whisper, so soft that it could barely be carried on a breath of air. "Have you come to dieeee?" An empty silence followed.

"Have you?" Brian growled defiantly. The next instant was blind pandemonium. Slippery creatures the size of small men lunged out of the white vapor. Brian's heart jumped, as the agile salamander-like fiends glommed onto him. Brian growled and flung one specter after another to the side.

With Smellinda at his back, he swatted them away with all his beastly strength. Smellinda was making a mess of them, crushing them and slapping them away as they came at her.

Brian moved forward taking the battle to them. He spun like a top with his sharp claws and huge arms moving like a windmill in a windstorm.

The monsters squealed in pain as he cut a path of destruction. He rapidly crushed the dark creatures as they hurled themselves at him. Some came up out of the bog, and still others jumped from trees. Scores of them splashed back into the muddy water broken and bleeding. Now he worked his way forward and crushed the barrage of shiny bodies. He shocked himself at the enormous growl that erupted from his throat, as he knocked his attackers back into the darkness.

The fierce fighters, too many to count, continued to close in. They bit and clawed and just kept coming. He felt himself starting to tire, and wondered how long he could withstand the endless assault. One specter managed to attach a suction-cupped finger to his temple, before Brian flung it aside.

Smellinda growled wildly and continued to destroy the frog-skinned things in the rapid-fire attack. Moving together in a tight circle, Brian and Smellinda began to turn the tide. They were now on the offensive, cutting through three or four of the specters at a time.

Brian spit the blood from his mouth, and then cursed himself for enjoying the taste. He flung the last leaping specter into the swamp and let out a thundering growl, "GRRAHHAAAAAAAAAAA!" Screaming into the abyss, he challenged anything that wanted to take him on.

All the chaos came to an abrupt halt. After a few moments of dead silence, Brian heard the chirp of a lone cricket, and then the croak of a frog. Slowly, the noise of insects and swamp creatures filled the air. Countless shiny-skinned bodies bobbed limply in the water, and then vanished beneath the surface, one by one.

Brian stared at Smellinda, who stood crunching on something in her mouth. She glanced back at him. "Graaahhhaaaa!" she bellowed, and then splashed a huge amount of swamp water into the air in triumph. She seemed content to sit in the bog and finish munching on the spoils of her victory.

Brian laid belly down in the black, still water and pushed himself along in the darkness with only his glowing eyes visible. Suddenly, hot panic surged through his body, and his heart quickened.

Sarah had been left alone during the entire fight.

"No one is back there to protect her," he thought, "For all I know this may have been a big diversion to get her alone. No! I don't want to think about what might have happened. Please, let me be wrong!"

The mud suctioned his legs, making quick movement difficult. Through the moonlit haze he could just make out a motionless dark shape leaning against the tree. "Must be her," he said with a sigh of relief.

As he moved in closer, he peered deeper into the mist and saw a streak of yellow moonlight slide along the shape's shiny body. "That's not Sarah!" He tried to yell, but the beast from within still had control and it came out, "Garrah!"

The slippery specter glanced in his direction. It scrambled off the grassy mound and quickly disappeared into the water. Brian clawed his way to where Sarah had been. Jumping out of the murky water, his chest landed on the turf. He pulled himself completely onto the mound of grass. On all fours he sniffed where Sarah had been. Then he dunked his entire head into the murky water. He couldn't see her; he couldn't smell her.

"I will take apart every inch of this horrible place until I find her," he thought. But he realized that if she had been taken into the swamp, finding her somewhere beneath the water would be impossible.

"She's missing and it's my fault!" Brian threw his head back in frustration, and slammed his huge fist into the grassy turf. "The beast took over while I slept, and I left her alone in this terrible place!"

Then he felt something eating into his temple. Reaching up he found part of a finger, with a suction cup on the end of it, attached to the side of his head. "Ewww!" He gave it a twist and it popped off. Blood trickled down his face and neck. "It has to be one of the specters' broken fingers. Obviously they aren't ghosts; they are flesh and blood."

Dumbfounded, Brian held the finger closer. It looked like eel skin, only it was black with dark green speckles. But then the rubbery skin changed color right before his eyes. It went from black to green, matching his own scales. He held it against the tree, and once again the finger changed color—this time matching the bark.

"The specters are like chameleons. And there must be thousands of them. I tore them up, but they kept coming and coming. Now that I think about it, they were trying like hell to stick their stupid suction-cup fingers to the side of my head."

"Greooow!" Smellinda hollered from a great distance through murky vapor.

"She's still calling them out. Hasn't she had enough? The specters must hide in the mist, and with their chameleon-like skin they can blend in with the colors of the trees," he thought. "No wonder everyone thinks they're ghosts—no one can see them. I can't be the first one to discover this. What scares me the most is that the secret has never left the swamp."

Brian raised his head and yelled, "Smellinda, get back here!"

Brian heard a terrible racket echoing from the bog. "The specters are going after Smellinda again," he thought. "She has to be tired by now."

He heard her growls and snaps mix with the specters' squeals and splashes. It rose to such intensity that he knew the battle was back in full swing. This time she was fighting them alone.

A moment later, he saw Smelinda's gray shape coming out of the bog. She had so many creatures clinging to her that she looked like a lumpy black mound moving through the water.

"Come on, girl!" Brian called out. "Get them off you. You can do it."

She let out an exhausted whimper. Just a moment before she was pulled beneath the water, Brian noticed that several fingers were attached to her temple. A few bubbles gurgled to the surface, and then Smellinda was gone.

Brian dropped to his knees and fell back in utter frustration. He lay numb and motionless for a moment. He felt a pin prick ever so lightly, like the bite of a spider on the right side of his head. His keen nose picked up the scent of something familiar. He heard the racing of another heart. In the same brief moment, he caught a glimpse of a spidery shadow, and realized it was a specter intertwined with the tree branch that hung above him. The specter had sharp teeth and a long fishy head.

"Aaah!" Brian screamed, waving his hands. He jerked forward with a start and popped the suction cup free. A green bead of beastly blood rolled down his face. In a moment of panic he snatched the specter's wrist and flung the creature over his head, sending it sprawling backwards.

"Squee!" wailed the specter, as it flopped like a rag doll head over heels in front him. Brian quickly grabbed the creature so it couldn't slip away into the swamp. The specter lay wiggling—its slippery head, skinny arms, and long slender tail exposed.

"You're next," it hissed.

"We shall see," Brian growled.

The specter's strange suction-cup fingers tightly gripped a geometric ball that hung from a loose strap around its neck. Brian knelt forward and put the weight of his knees onto the creature's shoulders. Then Brian snapped his teeth in anger and roared into the specter's face. "GRAAAA!" His chest puffed up and his pupils grew large. "What have you done with Sarah?"

The specter coughed and wrinkled its nose. "What's that smell?

"Where is the woman?"

The specter looked up at him and said nothing, as it clutched the orange-sized ball. Brian took hold of the small globe and looped it off the specter's neck. "Why do you want this thing so badly?" Brian dangled it in the air by its strap as the specter tried in vain to grasp it again.

"Give it to me! You have no use for it," whined the specter.

Brian snarled. "You know how to talk. Tell me where Sarah is."

The specter regarded him with its gleaming black eyes and trembled slightly. It grimaced, showing its small twin row of razor-sharp teeth.

Brian placed his entire weight over his knees, and the specter curled in pain.

"What does the ball do?" Brian asked.

"Memories—the ball opens them. We collect people— for their memories."

"How do you see memories?" Brian asked.

"The geo-ball is a memory projector. Every drop of blood contains an imprint of a memory. The ball lets us see it. We crave fresh blood and new memories. I look forward to taking yours."

"You will never see my memories. I will be getting out of this bog."

"No, you will never leave." The slippery creature's lips curved into a little smile. "There is no way out. No trick to learn. No clever maneuver to help you escape. Like the other beast, you will never leave here. I could lull you to sleep in a few moments by simply pressing my finger on your temple."

"Is that how you got Smellinda and Sarah?"

A jagged grin spread across the specter's thin lips.

Brian didn't like the creature's confidence. He suddenly felt vulnerable. He probed the area with his eyes for movement. "Where are your slippery friends?"

"You hurt them, and it has them a little shy for the time being."

"Take me to the woman and I'll let you go."

"I can take you to her, but you aren't going to like it. And I will never let you go."

Brian reached back and picked up the specter's long slithering tail. He wound it around his hand and pulled it taunt. "Let's make this simple. You take me to her now or I will twirl you over my head and slam you against the tree."

"Okay, but you must let me go regardless of what you might see."

Brian looped the strap from the geo-ball over his head with his free hand and hung the ball from his neck.

"Give me back the ball," squealed the creature.

"Sarah first," Brian growled.

The specter nodded, "Okay, get off me and then take a big breath."

Brian lifted his knees off the creature and let it slowly get back to its feet. Without warning the thing dove head-first into the swamp. Brian followed. An enormous splash resulted, as his great weight displaced the thick marsh. Brian held fast to the specter's tail and tried to keep up as it kicked and squirmed its way down into the thick mucky bottom.

The swirling dirt blinded Brian as they parted a tight network of roots loosely woven together. The specter clung onto a single taproot and pulled them even deeper into the bottom of the swamp. Brian forced his eyes open as the sediment began to thin. They were in a watery hole, still descending as the specter pulled his body hand over hand along the root. Then they curled upward into a big watery cave lined with sticks and roots. They swam for a time until their heads popped up inside of an air pocket. It was a small dome of trapped air resembling the inside of a beaver dam.

Brian pulled in a deep breath of air as he and the specter climbed out of the water. They ascended a pile of sticks toward an oval opening. All the while Brian kept a tight grip on the specter's tail.

From there they entered a huge maze of connecting tunnels. The tunnels were large enough that Brian was able to stand upright. The walls, speckled with water, were round and rubbery, and they pulsated and quivered with each step he took.

As they rounded the first turn, Brian caught a glimpse of Sarah. She was unconscious but breathing. Stuck up against the wall, she was held in place by a tight skin that covered everything but her head. Her face had a pale zombie-like appearance.

To her right, Smellinda, also unconscious, was attached to the wall. Beyond Smellinda the walls were lined on both sides with the hollow shells of pale victims that were stuck for all eternity with their blood drained dry.

Several creepy specters had attached their suction cups to Sarah and Smellinda. One of them was hanging upside down from the ceiling, operating a geo-ball. It had just manipulated a series of buttons when Brian and his still-captive specter guide entered. To Brian's amazement, the geo-ball sprang open, exposing optics and instrumentation.

"Get off her, you nasty spiders!" Brian yelled in an enormous fit of rage.

The specters froze and stared at him bug-eyed. Brian yanked his specter's tail and swung the creature like a hammer throw, using its body to knock the specters off Sarah and Smellinda. Brian managed to dislodge the creatures from the wall, but all of a sudden his specter's tail snapped off from the base with a loud pop! The creature twisted in pain. Brian used the leftover tail to whip the one on the ceiling across the head. "Squeee!" it cried, as it hit the wall and slid sideways. It scurried on all fours around a bend in the tunnel.

"I didn't mean to pull your tail off," Brian said to his specter. "But I can't say that I'm sorry about it either."

"We have a deal. Give me the geo-ball!" It reached with a quivering hand, as it lay on its side badly injured.

"Okay, you creepy blood-sucking salamander!"

Smellinda began to wake up. "Gerrrrmm," she purred. She groggily used her claws to dig into the thick skin that held her to the wall.

"You think you have won?" the specter said with a wicked sneer. "You may have your Sarah back, but you can never leave."

Smellinda shook off the last remnants of her catatonic state and thrust herself off the wall. She dove out and belly flopped hard on top of the specter, crunching its torso. "Eeee!" it squealed in a final surge of pain.

Brian jumped back and looked at the crushed specter with surprise. "I guess all bets are off then," he said to the specter. "If you're dead, then I'm keeping the geo ball and Sarah—but you can keep the tail." He tossed it onto the dead specter's face.

He moved quickly and used his claws to cut the skin that held Sarah. It dropped away, and he caught Sarah's limp body as she fell off the wall. He cradled her like a baby. "You're going to be okay," he said. "I'm not going to let these spidery eel-faces stop me."

Squeals echoed through the tunnel. "Sounds like

thousands of them," he said in a panic. He raced down the tunnel and instantly heard a clamoring behind him. He looked back and saw that the tunnel was dotted black with specters, all closing in. Some ran on the floor and walls, while others crawled upside down from the ceiling.

Sarah started to come to—groggily, at first. But suddenly she fully realized her predicament. "Please, please, keep them away from me!"

Smellinda was right on Brian's heels.

"Kill them all!" Brian yelled to her. "Kabata utta!"

Smellina smiled, exposing her white fangs like an angry tiger. Still somewhat dizzy, she stumbled slightly as she spun and charged back down the tunnel toward the specters.

Brian slipped Sarah over his shoulder and shouted, "Hang onto my back the best you can."

He felt her grip tighten as he bolted through the underground maze. Like a hamster in a tube, he scurried through the tunnels.

"Where are we going?" Sarah asked.

"I don't know, but we have to get there fast!" Running blindly along, he tried to take them farther away from the swamp. When he hit a dead-end, he began digging like a dog straight into the wall. He quickly cut through the rubbery side of the tunnel and made contact with wet clay. Mud and dirt flew behind him as he rapidly tunneled his way out.

Picking up a rhythm, he was able to dig at an upward angle like a mad dog possessed. He cut deep into clay and hit sand. Finally his claws struck rock. As he tore between jagged stones and rocks, pieces of his claws broke off. There was so much noise behind him he knew Smellinda was tearing the specters apart.

When Sarah began to slip off his neck, he reached back and righted her with his hand. Then he punched through a rock wall that opened into a large cavern. He glanced back, and even with his beastly ears he could barely make out the sound of the screeching specters.

He felt around in the gray darkness and found a boulder. He put his shoulder against it and rolled it to close off the tunnel he had just dug. Blinded by the darkness, he paused for a moment to catch his breath.

"You must have dug all the way up into Catacomb Caverns," Sarah gasped.

"I can't see anything. We could wander in here forever and not find our way out."

"Use your other senses."

"I can't taste my way out of here," he snapped. But then he sniffed the air. A fresh wave of cool air wafted through the moist cave stench. "I don't know much about caves but the best way to go must be up. The fresh air is coming through cracks in the ceiling rocks."

Brian moved forward, his nose in the air. Abruptly he hit his head on a low-level rock. He felt around, trying to see with his hands, like a blind person would. He found a jagged rock the size of a cow. Cautiously, he hefted the rock and rammed its tip into the flowing air overhead. The boulders shifted position with a rumble, but nothing else happened.

He growled and squatted. Then, with the rock poised in his upstretched hands, he pushed up with his powerful legs and bashed it into the overhead boulders again. Another rumble and the ceiling started to crumble away. He danced to the side, as rocks collapsed in front of them. A pencil-thin pillar of white light pierced the cavern above them. "Hey, are you still back there?" he said to Sarah.

"Yes! You did great! I know I haven't been saying much, but keep in mind that the specters paralyzed me and stole some of my blood. I'm still recovering, and it's all I can do to just hang on."

Brian nodded. "Got it. I won't expect any encouragement for a while." He ran a finger over his ragged claws, and put one of them into his mouth. Then he began chiseling it with his teeth back into a point.

On impulse he jumped up and dug his splintered claws into the rim of the opening above them. He was able to pull himself and Sarah up to the next level. A stream of light squeaked out of a small separation between a boulder and some smaller rocks. Brian took his thick palm and pressed the large brown rock overhead. It rose up slightly causing a flood of daylight to pour in. The light's brilliance blinded him for a moment.

He squinted and winced, as he pushed as hard as he could. He managed to lift one end of the rock and then tip it so that it rolled aside. "We're out!" he cried.

"You are fantastic. Let's see where we are," Sarah responded.

# CHAPTER TEN
# SHOWDOWN

BRIAN CLIMBED out of the cave with Sarah still clutching his back. He shielded his eyes from the bright morning sun. When he had moved the large boulder out of the way, he saw that it had left a six-foot wide nest-shape indentation. The small hole he had dug was in the very center.

As he looked around, he discovered they were in the middle of a "nest" of boulders. The hill around them was made mostly of red clay, with huge rocks covering it from top to bottom. The gaps between them were filled in by big, leafy blue-veined plants that grew from the soil.

Brian peeked over top of their fortress. Black Knights crawled like bugs all over the low-lying rocks as the sun dried the morning dew. They appeared to be working their way up the hill, gathering the big leaves. Some of them had small bundles of leaves in their arms; others carried the bigger bundles over their shoulders.

Brian gently placed Sarah on the ground to keep her hidden from view. Then he crouched and peered through a small opening between two massive boulders. He spotted Leether moving about in a flat area at the bottom of the hill.

"Leether's got a fire going," he whispered to Sarah.

"What's he doing?" Sarah asked groggily.

He pointed to a nearby plant. "He's squeezing oil from the blue leaves into a big vase."

"He's getting ready for a ceremony. This is not good."

"If the knights keep moving up the hill, they will eventually find us and alert Leether," warned Brian.

"At least Leether doesn't know that we're here right now, or he would be on us in a moment."

Sarah didn't look much better than when he had taken her from the wall. Blood still oozed from her left temple. Brian knelt next to her and dug a little muddy clay from between the rocks and pressed it against her head to slow the bleeding. Then he plucked a large leaf still wet with morning dew. Cradling her head, he poured the few drops of liquid into her mouth. The moisture seemed to loosen the back of her throat, and her eyes cleared slightly.

"Leether is setting up to finally put an end to us," she said. "Let me think this thing through. He has the knights picking the leaves to make blue leaf oil."

Brian said, "I remember lighting that blue oil when I escaped from the castle. It works on the cloud like catnip does to a cat."

"He will wait until we show up before he lights the oil. I bet he plans to sacrifice us right here."

"He must plan for every possibility," said Brian. "He can finally have his justice. I saw a few ropes at the bottom of the hill. He'll tie us down, light the oil, and wait for the cloud to swoop in and devour us. I'm tired of running from him," Brian snarled.

"This is it for me, too," said Sarah. "I can't run anymore. He will chase us the rest of our days. I have one more fight left in me. If I can rest a bit, maybe I can pull it together.

Before I fight him, I must have one more thing."

"What?"

"Snow. He is supposed to be with me at the end. We made a pact. We mixed our blood into a cup of wine and both drank from it. I swore on my soul that we would go down together. He needs to be here. Consider it my dying wish."

"But we'll be discovered soon. The knights are working their way up the hill."

Just then they heard a quiet snort, and a bumpy little gerbit scampered between the rocks and stood above them looking down. "Snort, snort," it said, as it twitched its snoot.

"Ebil's gerbit! How did it find us?" Sarah exclaimed. "Look! It has something." She pointed to a tightly rolled leather scroll firmly clamped between its teeth.

Brian scooped up the little porker and set it down softly on the ground behind the rocks. Sarah took the scroll from the gerbit's mouth and unrolled it. "It is a note from Snow!" She touched the writing with her index finger and rubbed the dark red ink between her fingers. "This is written in blood."

"Who writes in blood?" Brian realized that had sounded somewhat insensitive. Obviously she was very concerned for her friend's welfare. He tried to console her. "Maybe he didn't have a pencil. I mean, out here what are you supposed to write with?"

"It says, 'Sarah, I hope you are still alive to read this. I want you to know I have done all I can to be with you. I have fought within a whisker of death to be there. If you can only hold out a little longer I…" There was a scrawl after the last word that sharply cut across the leather cloth.

She began to cry. "Why didn't he finish it? Something got him!" Sarah grabbed the pig's face and held it still so it could peer into her eyes and hopefully understand what she was about to say. "How did you know where to find us? Where is Snow? Can you take a note back to him?"

"Snort, snort, gunort," said the gerbit, nodding.

Sarah smiled. "He understands! At least, I think he understands."

The pig began walking in a tight circle, almost nose to tail.

"What's he doing?" Brian asked.

"He's thinking. Gerbits probably spin to clear their little piglet brains."

The chubby little pig spun several times, and then lay down and nuzzled his snout into the loose dirt for a nice nap.

Sarah frowned.

Brian sniffed the note, "The blood on the note is still fresh. If Snow is alive, he's not too far away."

"Hey, the specters loaded my blood into that geometric ball to see my memories. Maybe it will work on just a little of the blood from Snow's note so we can see what happened to him."

Brian held the geo-ball. "It's a strange device. I haven't had time to play with it. I think its shape is called a polyhedron. I can't remember exactly. I only got a C-plus in geometry. This ball is made up of little pentagons all linked together."

Sarah leaned back against a rock and took the ball from around Brian's neck. "It reminds me of a puzzle ball," she said, as she brushed off the dirt with her fingers. She pushed one of the pentagon-shaped panels on the side and it popped open like a pocket watch. She pushed another panel and that lid also popped open.

"Push them all," said Brian.

She pushed each panel, and each one clicked, flipped open, and snapped into place. They each revealed something different, from delicate clocklike instrumentation and mirrors to glass prisms and optics. She pushed the final panel on the top, and it disappeared inside the ball making a geometric hole. She held the tangled shape of mirrors and optics in her palm.

"What's that?" asked Brian. He observed a round soapy-looking bubble growing out of the hole at the top of the ball. It looked like any other soap bubble with beautiful swirling colors of blue, yellow, and purple. But this bubble grew to the size of a melon.

"Pretty," said Sarah. "I wonder if it is just for looks, like a bubble pipe."

"It's fancy and all, but it is hard to believe it doesn't do more than that," Brian said, as he stared into the swirling shapes. He hoped for some kind of sign or secret message, but it was just a very large pretty blue bubble.

"I'm going to squeeze a drop of blood onto the bubble and see what happens," Brian said. He picked up the leather note and used his great strength to wring out one large drop of bright red blood. When the blood hit the bubble, the colors spread and formed a swirling globe of red and purple.

The pattern was indistinct at first, but eventually it cleared and an image emerged. "It's working!" said Sarah. "It's as if we're looking through Snow's eyes!"

Knuckles slammed into Snow's face as a young boy. His head snapped back and the ground came up to meet him. "Stay down, Snow glow!"

Snow looked up and raised his fist in defiance. Then a barrage of lefts and rights continued to rain down on him.

"You're way too far back in his memories," said Brian. "We need recent history."

"Well I don't know how to fast forward." She tapped the ball with her palm and shook it hard. There was a blur of action, and the image cleared again. This time it showed Snow at the Pit of Despair. "This was the last time we saw him," Sarah said.

They heard Snow say, "We will meet at the base of the rocky hill. And I still think he said 'nasty' not 'Cassie'..."

Sarah stared wide-eyed at the geo-ball as it continued to reveal what happened next. Her face flushed, as she observed the recent memories of her friend.

Together, Sarah and Brian watched. They saw Snow and Ebil being pursued by a platoon of knights, as they ran from the clearing during the start of the battle. Zebra-striped natives captured them and put them in an arena where they battled the knights for the natives' entertainment. They were able to escape, but as Snow wrote the note, they heard a loud shriek and all went black. The once-beautiful bubble popped.

"Oh no!" Sarah cried. "That's how it ends?"

Her hands fell limp. The geo-ball dropped into her lap. "Snow probably died while trying to write the note. The natives must have caught up with him."

"Quiet!" shushed Brian.

A knight said, "Hey, what was that? Who's hiding up there?"

"Now you've done it," Brian growled. "They heard you and are coming up here. What are we going to do?"

Sarah looked down into the dark cavern. "I can tell you that I'm not going back into that awful hole to escape them. I'd rather fight the knights right here than risk seeing a specter ever again."

"Aren't you afraid of the knights, too?" Brian asked.

"Maybe I am, but I'm thinking that they are more afraid of you."

Brian spied several knights, carrying bundles of blue leaves on their backs, coming directly toward them. He heard an evil cackle and peeked out. Leether seemed to be enjoying the fire that he had worked into a raging inferno. He smiled and leaned back as the flames tried to lick him. Then he turned and stroked the top of a black box that sat on a large rock next to him.

"That box is sitting right out in the open," whispered Brian. "The aura of the wind spirit Eurus is still inside the glass ball, and the glass ball is inside the box!"

"Leether had you trapped that same way, didn't he?"

"Yeah, you got it right. Then the beast ate the ball and that's how my aura became trapped inside this body. I hated it in that glassy ball, and I was only trapped for a few minutes. I want to run down there right now, grab the box, and crush Leether into dust! I can't imagine what it must be like for Eurus to be entombed in a little glassy ball for so long."

Brian's ear twitched. He heard the mumblings of the two knights as they neared the top of the hill.

"I'm sure I heard a woman's voice," said the first knight. "And you know a woman was seen traveling with the green beast. Leether said they would be here soon. He's completely and utterly obsessed about them for reasons unknown."

"Ours is not to question the will of Nimbus," said the second knight. "Leether knows, and that is good enough for me. Where did that voice come from?"

Sarah whispered, "We'll be discovered in a few moments. What's the plan?"

"We need to weaken Leether in order to have a chance," said Brian.

"If we can separate Leether from the cloud, I bet you can beat him one on one."

Their conversation was interrupted when they saw the spikes of a black helmet slowly appearing over the rocks. The spikes' pointed shadows crawled across the boulders behind them. One of the knights peeked cautiously over the stones and looked directly into the venomous black slits in Brian' eyes. The knight trembled with fear and his mouth dropped open. "Aaahhh!" he cried out.

Brian grabbed the knight's helmet between his claws and cracked it solidly against the rocks. The knight's body went limp.

The second knight was so startled that he tumbled backward. His armor could be heard clanking off several rocks as he ricocheted down the hill. He came to rest between several boulders. "The beast!" he yelled, as he desperately tried to get up. "Help! Up here! I found the green beast!"

Brian snuck a quick look over the top of a smooth boulder and saw Leether's head spin, as if on a swivel. His red eyes stared like lasers and locked onto Brian's.

Leether thrust his staff into the air and beckoned loudly, calling to his cloud god. "Misty monsters, phantom core, take these vermin to death's door. Rufescent, phantom, ghost-like brume, cast your haze…"

At once the red cloud appeared over the trees. The orange-red blob expanded into a quivering mass that measured a hundred yards across, and it bowed to its dark master.

"It all ends now," said Sarah "And I am fine with it. I may join Skaht and Snow in death, but I will have the satisfaction of taking my best shot at that gruesome maniac on my way out! Snow would call this a real clasher-basher. I have just enough strength left to go at it one last time."

Brian detected a hissing sound coming from the cave below. He knelt on the rocky ground and forced his eyes to peer into the dark tunnel beneath his feet. There was so much movement; it was like staring into a swarm of black ants. "It's the specters, and they're filling the cave below us!"

"Well, then they got past Smellinda," Sarah said. "And

they found a way into the tunnel. No doubt there are many different paths to get through the caverns."

"Quick—light up some leaves and drop them into the hole," said Brian. "The cloud will follow the smoke into the cave."

Sarah nodded. She quickly took the tight bundle of blue leaves from the unconscious knight's back. Fumbling for her flint and finally retrieving it, she frantically worked to spark some of the oil on the leaves.

Brian blew small puffs on the tiny yellow flame. It began to glow brighter. When Brian paused for another breath, the entire bundle whooshed with fire. Blue smoke poured out of the large bundle of leaves and stung his eyes.

Sarah coughed and grinned as she stood on top a rock and waved the leaves in one big circle over her head. "Over here, Nimbus," she yelled. She threw them into the hole.

"Eeeeeeeee!" Hundreds of specters choked and squealed as the smoke billowed into the connecting caverns and rose out of the hole in a twisting pillar of blue-gray smoke.

Brian watched as the cloud lifted and caught the scent of fresh smoke. "Get clear!" Brian yelled.

He and Sarah scrambled from their hiding place and slid over the top of the rocks on their bellies. The cloud elongated as it stretched toward the hill.

In a moment, the tip of the blobby cloud began threading itself into the hole. The specters scurried through the underground tunnels like rats.

"Noooooooooo!" Leether cried in frustration. He pounded the end of his scepter on the ground.

In mere moments, the last bit of cloud vanished into the caverns. Brian pressed his shoulder against the same large boulder he had lifted out of the cave and rolled it back into the hole. It landed snugly with a solid thud, sealing the tunnel like a ten-ton cork.

"Yes! Yes!" Sarah yelled. Unable to contain her excitement she jumped onto Brian's lumpy back and patted him on the side of his scaly face.

Brian's thrill was short-lived when he spotted dozens of knights ascending the hill in an effort to get them.

"I'm going after Leether, right now," Brian growled. "Are you with me?"

"Yes! Let's go get him. Quick, before Nimbus finds a way out of the cave."

"Hang on tight," Brian said, and he sprang down the rocks.

The knights came at him but were knocked off their feet as he bounded past them. They fell backward, like bowling pins, over the rocks before coming to rest, beaten and battered. It was no contest.

Leether held his staff like a giant lighting rod and faced Brian.

Brian leapt from rock to rock, leaving a path strewn with wrecked knights in his wake. Suddenly, Brian felt a sharp pain. He looked at his side, where a spear protruded. "Agh!" he yelped, and broke the spear off at its base. "I forget these little guys can actually hurt me."

He spotted the quaking knight who, despite being knocked down and wedged between two boulders, had managed to stick Brian with his spear. The frightened knight cowered and ducked but could not free himself. Brian jumped down and stood on the rock directly above him.

The knight took off his helmet and dropped his sword. "I give up! Take Leether, just don't kill me," he pleaded.

Brian spread his arms out wide like a sumo wrestler preparing to battle. His broken yellow claws flexed from his fingertips and his chest puffed up. Massive amounts of blood shot through every fiber of his body, and his anger exploded into a huge GROOOOW that shattered the frazzled nerves of every knight pursuing him. Even Leether took a step back, and, for the first time, Brian saw doubt in his eyes.

Bypassing the terrified knight, Brian jumped onto a large boulder at the bottom of the hill and used it as a springboard to catapult high into the air.

With both arms wrapped around Brian's neck, Sarah squeezed tight. The ground quaked as Brian landed in a flat area of ground directly in front of Leether.

"Attack!" Leether shouted, as he waved his staff over his head. But any knights that had not been shattered in Brian's path had lost their nerve.

Sarah sat tall on Brian's back, pointed at Leether, and screamed, "They won't give their lives for you! Without the cloud backing you up, what are you? They already see it's over. You won't be lording over them ever again."

"Now!" Leether bellowed at the knights. His thunderous voice shook the air. The knights glanced at each other uneasily, but still did not move to his defense.

Brian smiled with satisfaction. One of his fangs protruded from his upper lip. "Come here, you gruesome psychopath," he said, waving Leether in.

"Sarah, get the black box," Brian said under his breath.

Sarah slid off Brian's back and ran for the box. Leether moved toward her, but Brian leaped to the side and blocked his path.

"No, it's just you and me," Brian growled, his pupils enlarging. He mirrored Leether's every move.

Leether tilted his head slightly and sneered at Sarah. "I thought that was you!"

Brian was surprised at Sarah's reaction. She cowered self-consciously and dipped her head like a timid rabbit. The black box shook in her trembling hand.

Leether continued brashly, "Sarah, it's been a long time. You have really let yourself go. Ha-ha! Had a couple of rough days, have you? And where are those two idiots who left with you when you were banished? Ran off when the going got tough? I thought so."

Sarah remained transfixed as she held onto the black box.

Leether continued, "Tell me how it feels to have everyone think you're dead for all these years. Tell you what. For old time's sake, I will give you a ten-minute head start if you carefully set that box back down and run for the hills. As for your daughter—remember her? The one you never met? She turned out to be quite a little brat. I left a little of myself behind in the other world to take care of her, so ponder that while you flee. She was designated for sacrifice, just like the kid inside this green monster. It has so been decreed."

Brian stared at Sarah. "What will she do?" he thought. "Will she save herself and run for it while she has a chance?"

He watched as her face hardened. Then she glanced at him and grinned. "Brian, kill him…kill him a lot!" she barked.

Brian lunged at Leether with his jaws wide.

However, Leether spun and dropped to one knee, while skillfully rotating the scepter up. In a flash, he used the scepter to push the barbed end of the spear tip that protruded from Brian's side, deep into his abdomen.

Brian buckled and howled in pain. But he gritted his teeth, and with an enormous backhand, sent Leether flailing into the unforgiving rocks.

Leether's body took the full impact, and he crumpled to the ground. A trickle of blood dribbled from his ear. Then he righted himself, held his staff in the air, and began to chant, "Rufescent phantom ghost-like brume…" Red mist emerged from the golden ball on top of his scepter.

Brian laughed. "The cloud can't save you now. The next time I come at you I will put your lights out."

Leether shook his head and sneered. "I will never succumb to the likes of you. You are the dirt between my toes. You are but an ugly spider to be stepped on. You can't fight your destiny. Justice will be done for Nimbus!"

A rumble growled beneath the earth. Then thunder shook the inner caverns, and the ground began to quake.

"Quit yacking and finish him before the cloud pushes its way out of the cave," Sarah yelled. As if to validate her warning, the hill trembled. A few small rocks shook loose and tumbled down the hill.

Once again, Brian snarled and charged at Leether. As Brian neared, Leether broke a small glass tube between his palms and flung a misty red powder into Brian's face.

His eyes burning, and unable to see, Brian swung wildly and caught the top of Leether's head, knocking him to the ground. Then Brian flopped onto his back and rolled in pain, as the mist burned into his eyes and lungs. He coughed and gagged, but the searing pain kept increasing, burning into him like hot coals.

Leether laughed maniacally as he staggered toward the great fallen beast and shoved the scepter's golden ball into Brian's wide nostril. Red mist rose from the ball and seeped into Brian's nose. "Justice will be done!" Leether roared.

Brian choked and tried to raise his arms, but they had become too heavy to lift.

The ground rumbled once again. Brian glanced toward the hill and noticed a slimy black specter peeking out of the cracks between the boulders.

Brian tried to growl, but his strength was gone. He had to somehow revive the beast inside him—the same beast he had worked so hard to repress. He forced a growl and felt a small surge of energy. It gave him just enough strength to swing his limp arm at Leether and knocked him away.

Brian's eyes burned, but he forced them open. From where he was laying he could see Sarah had taken the glassy ball out of the black box and was trying to fit the entire thing into her small mouth. "Brian, how do I eat this thing?" she cried "I need the wind spirit's powers to save you!"

Brian looked at her blankly not knowing what to say.

Just then, a slippery specter squealed and shot out from a jagged crack between the ground-level rocks. It had an elongating glob of cloud goo still attached to one arm. The specter jerked its arm free from the cloud's sticky grasp. The goo snapped back but continued oozing out from the cracks in the rocks.

The specter scurried like a spider and quickly glommed onto Sarah's back. She cringed as it hung over the top of her head looking at her upside down. As the specter attached itself to her temple, it opened its mouth in excitement, exposing its twin row of frightening teeth. On impulse, Sarah shoved the glassy ball into its mouth with one hand, and punched up hard under its chin with her forearm. Its eyes widened, and it shook as if from an inner earthquake. It fell back off Sarah, struggled to stand, and then stood upright.

Leether laughed out loud. "That was wonderful! Now Eurus will spend eternity inside a slimly specter. Isn't that marvelous? I couldn't have thought of a more fitting end to him."

In a fit of rage, Sarah charged the much larger Leether, and connected a right cross to his jaw. Leether merely grinned and laughed off the blow. He grabbed a handful of her long hair and twisted it in his hand. With a loud grunt, he whipped her over his shoulders and then slammed her to the ground. She convulsed and lay motionless.

The staggering specter blinked and raised its eyebrows, as if to see clearly for the first time. It looked down at its shiny body and examined its suctioned-cupped fingers. Then it glanced at Brian, caught his eye, and winked.

Leether stood over the fallen Brian and reveled in his victory. But Brian, using the last of his strength, reached out and wrapped his reptilian fingers tightly around Leether's ankle. Leether bent right over Brian's face and laughed. "How futile are your efforts now," he said.

But his victorious expression turned to one of surprise when Brian spat the burning mist straight into Leether's face. He yelped as he reeled backward, clutching his burning eyes.

The opportunistic specter sprang onto Leether's shoulders and quickly attached both its hands to either side of Leether's temples.

The red cloud continued to ooze from between the cracks in the rocks. Then the segments merged and soared into the sky.

Leether tried to raise his staff, but it was too late. His eyes rolled back into his head, leaving only the whites visible.

The specter grinned. "Squeeeeee!"

"Eurus, you in there?" Brian asked.

"Yessss," hissed the specter. "I am free. Squueee!"

Countless specters heeded his call. They swarmed out of the cracks and scampered toward Leether. Soon, Leether was no longer visible beneath the pile of squirming creatures. They hissed wickedly and squealed as they dragged Leether's limp body toward the boulders. They pulled him up and then lifted him sideways, taking him head first into the caverns. His feet were the last things to disappear.

Eurus was about to slither out of sight between the rocks. As if realizing that he forgot to say good-bye, he turned his slippery head and gave a childlike wave before vanishing into the hill.

Brian smiled and nodded. Then he returned his attention to the swirling cloud of red goo that was forming overhead.

"Who's your master now?" Brian called out, while still on his back. He rubbed his burning eyes and reached for Leether's twisted staff that had been left in the dirt. He wrapped his fingers around it and threw it hard and high into cloud's mass. The cloud roared and the air crackled with lightning. Then it unloaded an angry rainstorm as it lifted itself high over the rocky hill.

Brian opened his eyes and mouth wide. He felt the rain cool the fire that burned inside him. "You have no brain and you have no master," he shouted angrily. "Who is going to think for you now?"

The cloud continued to rise. Brian got to one knee and, finally, managed to stand in the drenching rain. He staggered to Sarah who still lay motionless in the dirt. He knelt next to her and listened. He detected a shallow heartbeat but no breathing. He gently cupped the back of her head with his big paw and placed his large jaws over her mouth, careful to keep his sharp teeth back. And he blew life into her lungs.

Her eyes fluttered.

Without warning, a searing pain shot through his scaled back like a hot bolt of lightning. He looked down and saw the tip of a razor sharp blade jutting from his belly. The blade twisted abruptly, sending a horrible pain pulsing through his entire body.

He heard someone yell from behind, "I got him, Sarah!"

"Snow," Brian thought. "Snow is killing me! Where did he come from?"

Brian grabbed the icy blade to keep it still, but Snow quickly yanked it back out, slicing through several of Brian's fingers.

Then Brian felt a dull thump, as the handle of Snow's sword slammed into the back of his head. Brian slumped to the ground semiconscious and dying. Despite feeling numb, Brian had never been more aware of what was happening around him.

"What are you doing to her, you filthy monster?" Snow screamed, standing over Brian's beastly body.

Sarah began to stir. When she was finally able to sit up, she yelled, "Oh no! Snow, what have you done?"

"What have I done? Ebil and I just fought knights in a crazy battle arena of death, and then escaped from hundreds of angry natives just to get here to save you. I was nice enough to write you a note, but that anxious gerbit grabbed it and ran before I could finish."

"You idiot!"

"Idiot? Do you have any idea how many times I cheated death just to get here?" Snow looked down and started counting on his fingers. "One, two, three…"

"You just killed a special person…so don't expect gratitude!" She knelt next to Brian and clutched his damp face as she cried.

"Person?"

"Yes, person. He was a good person. He wasn't trying to hurt me. He has been good and loyal—and smart! Now you have killed him! Why must you always strike first and think later?"

Snow sounded as if he was tearing up. "I…I had no choice. You only get one chance to kill a beast. It has to be by complete and utter surprise. If they see it coming, it is game over…and I was so sure I was doing the right thing! I thought he was eating your face off."

Ebil sat quietly on a rock behind them taking it all in.

"You will see that the beast is better off dead. Just open its eyes and lift its head."

Sarah tilted Brian's heavy, oversized head toward her and pulled back his thorny eyelids. She looked deep into his eyes. They were dull and black. "Brian…Brian, are you still in there?"

Snow threw his arms up in utter frustration and took a big breath. "Will you ever forgive me?"

Sarah looked at him through tear-filled eyes. "I don't know if I can right now. I don't know."

Then she saw just a glint of smoke rising like steam from the center of the beast's eyes. It was faint at first, but it gave way to a darker form.

Sarah smiled. "He's not dead!"

The smoke continued to rise, and as it condensed, it began to take shape. She could make out the form of a young man. It looked like a hazy ghost.

She gasped. "Now I can see you! Is that your aura? You are actually quite a good looking kid, aren't you?"

Brian was elated to once again be in his aura state. Snow, as it turned out, couldn't have done him a bigger favor. "Whoa!" said Brian. He felt a strange force pulling him away.

"Something has got him! Get something to collect him in!" she said in panic.

"No," said Brian. "Leether can't hurt us anymore. This is a good thing. It feels more like a mother leading a child by the hand."

Slipping away with the wind, he let the gentle force take him. As he was whisked along, he brushed against the rocks and back through the dangling moss of the swamp.

He heard a soft voice. It was barely audible. Then he heard it again. It was gentle and kind. The sound warmed him like the first sip of hot chocolate on a winter morning.

"Brian," said the voice.

"Grandma? Is that you?"

"I have stalled going to the ever-after. I am somewhere in between." She began to take on a misty form.

"Are you an aura?"

"I am not an aura, I am a ghost or an angel, or I guess you could say an angel's ghost. Yes, I like that. I am an angel's ghost."

"Angel's ghost?"

"You must get home quickly, dear. They are about to take your body. It is important for you to realize that you only have a few moments to spare. Now hurry, wonderful grandson, and be quick about it! Fate has given you the chance to stay alive, but making it happen is up to you. I have watched you for as long as I can, but my time in the in-between is growing very thin."

Brian wanted to hug her, but he knew he shouldn't hesitate, and it probably wouldn't work anyway. He headed toward the membrane in a flash. In just a few moments, Specters Fog and Sarah were just small dots behind him.

He cleared the mountains and glanced at the ghastly twisted castle below. Red mist rose off the Valley of Tears as the landscaped changed back to sunlit grasses.

Swooping low, he came upon the black membrane, still fractured with cloud goo. He formed into a thin spiral and glided through the gooey crack and back into the dark tunnel. He seeped through the hole in the bottom of the pond and floated toward the shimmering sunlight above. He broke through the surface of the pond without as much as a ripple, and sped for home.

"I can't wait to see Cassie!" he rejoiced.

# CHAPTER ELEVEN
# THE HOMECOMING

BRIAN FOUND it very satisfying to float over the checkered farmlands below. "What happened while I was gone?" he wondered. "It looks like the sun has just set."

He observed the last speck of a glowing orange sun on the horizon. He sped over the beautifully lit countryside until he spotted his familiar farmhouse. Just the sight of home sent an excited chill through him. Diving down, he slipped though the walls of the house as easily as a breeze drifts through an open window.

He entered his bedroom and hovered for a moment over the neglected body that lay there, still as a stone. To his horror, a white sheet covered his head. He heard muffled voices in the other room. "One voice is definitely Mom's," he thought. "I don't recognize the others."

He couldn't wait to get back into his old skin. He imagined it would feel like putting on a comfortable pair of pajamas right out of the dryer. Letting his ghostly aura fall gently toward his physical form, it wavered for a moment and then settled into place.

As it locked into his body, he felt a sudden surge of pain

like he had never experienced before in his life. His dormant muscles began to spasm and lock up. His eyes fluttered at first, and then he managed a solid blink. He strained but couldn't even wiggle his fingers. With tremendous effort, he opened his mouth to call out, but his throat was as dry as a dusty riverbed.

"My body is a mess," he thought.

He heard two people walk into the room and the door close firmly behind them. All he could do was lay motionless and stare at the white sheet that covered his face.

"This is ridiculous," said a man with a deep voice. "I asked her when was last time she checked to see if he was breathing and she just stared at me."

"When I got here he was obviously dead. I got nothing on his carotid."

"I'm glad you called me right away. I'll pronounce him, but how long do you think this kid has been laying here? Not only is he ice cold, his body is as hard as granite. Have you ever encountered anything like this?"

"I've been a paramedic for many years but have never come across a body in this condition."

"Well, as a medical examiner, I would like to give an exact time of death. But this one will be a puzzler."

"Do you think we have a case of criminal neglect?"

"Maybe, there is something very abnormal about this whole scenario."

Brian's entire body ached as his heart made its first shallow ba-bump. Then it beat again, this time stronger and smoother. It started pumping more rhythmically, missing a beat here and there, and then smoothing out. It reminded Brian of someone trying to start a rusty old tractor engine that hadn't been fired up for years.

A radio squawked. "Unit 41, we have a two-car injury

accident at Westland and Five Mile. Are you clear?"

"Yeah, 41 has it. I will be clearing here shortly."

"I am going to find out what happened here," the medical examiner said. He reached his hand under the sheet and found the carotid artery on Brian's neck. "Okay, let's make this official. No respiration and no…. What? Wait a minute, am I feeling my own pulse?"

He yanked the sheet back, and Brian looked up at him.

"Whoa!" The medical examiner jerked back.

Brian took his first breath. It felt like a desert cavern had opened up and the air was rushing in to fill the void.

The medical examiner gawked at him, wide-eyed. "Holy cow! Did you see that?" He put the back of his hand on Brian's cheek. "He's getting warmer, and look, he's pinking up!"

"Unbelievable!" said the paramedic. "You ready to proclaim a miracle?"

The medical examiner shook his head. "No—that's not in my job description, but I'm ready to go have a drink and start early retirement. I don't even know what I am doing anymore." He put his hand on Brian's chest and felt it rise and fall. "Can you hear me, Brian?"

Brian tried to talk but his vocal cords were so dry it came out, "Yaiieee."

Someone fumbled with the doorknob, and then the door sprang open as his mother burst into the room. "Brian? Was that my Brian?"

Brian blinked, and his mother dove on him. She wrapped her arms tightly around him, laughing and then crying—all at the same time.

Tommy appeared on the other side of the bed. "Brian?" Tommy gripped Brian's head and turned it toward him. Bending down only inches from his brother's face, Tommy peered deep into his eyes. When they made eye contact, Tommy grinned. "Yup! He's in there!"

"Geesh, let him breath," said the paramedic.

"Iiiiiiiieeee," said Brian.

"Quick, get him some water! He's trying to talk to us," said Mom.

Tommy handed her a water bottle from the nightstand while the medical examiner and paramedic took a step back. She lifted his head and trickled the cool water into his mouth. With great concentration he managed to swallow. The rush of cool liquid washed against the inside of his larynx.

He cleared his throat, "Um…Cassie?"

"Gone," said Tommy. "She went back after you!"

"What? Why?"

"You promised us you would be back by breakfast, and that was like a week ago!"

The paramedic gently nudged Tommy to the side and took up Brian's wrist. Glancing down at his watch he began to take a pulse.

Mom's eyes began to tear. "That girl …she was in here holding your hand all day, every day. I even brought food in to her because she wouldn't leave the room. I told her that I didn't think you were ever coming back and that she had to face it. It was then that I decided it was time to call an ambulance. She got really upset. She said if you wouldn't come back to her, she would go to you. She thought she might know a way to do it."

"Pulse 64 strong and steady," smiled the paramedic in disbelief.

Mom ran her fingers through Brian's hair. "God knows that girl loves you." A tear broke free from one of her eyes and slid down her cheek. "When I got off the phone she was gone. I went looking for her but didn't have any luck."

"I have got to go after her," Brian rasped. "There's no getting through the membrane! She could easily drown just trying to get down there!"

Brian tried to sit up but merely listed forward. He tried to raise his arms. But the pain was too much.

"Whoa!" said the paramedic placing a hand on Brian's chest, "The only place you're going is the hospital."

Mom nodded.

A vibrating hum interrupted the paramedic. He clicked on his cell phone. "Yup, I know. Okay, yes…fifteen minutes. Correction, no human remains here. No, he came back to life. No, actually I'm not joking."

Brian tried again to sit up. The world began to whirl into a blurry haze and Brian passed out. He woke up in the hospital, a web of wires and machines attached to him. Brian turned his head. His mom was sitting at his side.

"Just relax," she said. "They're checking you out. So far, your heart, lungs, brain, etcetera looks good. The bad news is that you have atrophy. Your muscles and bones…they are really stiff."

"I wish I had a tub of yellow fluid like they use in the other world," said Brian. "I would be as good as new in about a half hour."

"They suggest we see our family doctor to see what can be done."

They spent the entire night at the hospital, and the next morning, after everything checked out, they released Brian. Mom, Brian, and Tommy returned home just before sunrise.

At the house Brian said, "Hey, do we still have Grandma's wheelchair?"

"Sure. Why?" said Tommy.

"Can you push me to the pond?"

"Now? Are you kidding? You just got back home. And

it's awfully bumpy on the path. But I guess I could do it. What if I accidentally dump you out of the chair?"

"Then you pick me up and put me back in. I'm not a piece of china. Better yet, just run me into the wall so I can break my aura out of this crappy body and go look for her."

"No!" said Mom firmly. "That is not going to happen. I just got you back. Your body is barely functional as it is. You will not have a body to come back to if you keep leaving it behind. And besides, I told you that I already went looking for her. I found her shoes on the shore and footprints going into the water. There was no other sign of her."

"Take me there!" Brian demanded. "I want to see for myself. I can't lose her like this!"

"If you want to go to the pond then I will take you there," said Tommy.

Mom rolled her eyes and blew air out of her puffed cheeks in exasperation. But she helped Tommy transport Brian's dead-weight body into the wheelchair.

Once Brian was firmly seated in the chair, Tommy pushed him through the house. Mom trailed close behind.

As they moved through the kitchen, Brian saw a half-eaten cake with candles on it. "Have a party?"

"You missed your birthday. It was kind of weird without you there. Happy birthday, brother."

Brian looked puzzled. "I missed my birthday and it never even occurred to me." He grimaced and flexed his fingers then slowly rotated his stiff neck.

Tommy maneuvered the wheelchair through the breezeway, out the squeaky screen door, and into the backyard.

At the pond, Brian noticed the small wooden boat adrift in the still water. Tommy pushed Brian to the edge of the sloped grassy bank. The bank had a steep angle, and the shore dropped straight away into the deepest part of the pond. Brian leaned forward to peer into the water.

"This is where I picked up her shoes," Mom said, pointing. "They were sitting right here behind this bush."

Brian looked at the delicate webbed footprints in the muddy bank. "Yup, those are her footprints for sure. See that?" He pointed at the smooth divot next to her shoes. "It looks like there was a good-sized rock there."

"What would she have needed the rock for?" Mom asked.

Brian thought a moment. "Maybe she used it as a weight so she'd sink faster to the bottom of the pond. She's pretty resourceful."

"How would she get through the membrane?" asked Tommy.

"I don't know. Even if she found the hole in the bottom of the pond and got into the tunnel, she would be stuck down there. The membrane is now hard and black with some of the cloud trapped in the middle of it. Remember when I threw the crystal into the pond to close the doorway? Well, the cloud was caught halfway to Aphelion Chiasm."

"Aphelion Chiasm?"

"Remember, that's what Cassie calls her world. Part of the cloud went back and part stayed here. The middle of it is trapped in the membrane."

"I know what you're thinking," Tommy said. He raised one eyebrow. "You can hardly move a muscle, so it's my turn. I should go down there and get her."

"No, that is not what I was thinking at all."

"No," said Mom sternly.

"I want to do it!" Tommy lifted his leg and pulled off his shoe. He flipped it over his shoulder.

As he began taking off his shirt, his mother grabbed him. "No! You are not!"

"Stop it! Let go of me! I did it once, and I can do it again!"

Then Brian noticed a bubble pop on the pond's surface. "Look!" he said, and he pointed at a ripple that grew from the center of the pond toward the shoreline. A fizzing of smaller bubbles followed.

Tense moments passed, and yet nothing else happened. The morning sunlight cut through the trees and sliced through the water, which helped them see into the depths.

Brian's heart sank when he observed a blurry red blob streaking upward like an angry red rocket. It erupted like a volcano, leaving a trail of water as it broke through the surface. In the next moment it was gone.

Mom clasped her face in shock as the cloud streaked by her.

Tommy let go of the wheelchair, and it rolled down the sloped bank.

"Tom, help!" Brian yelled, as the chair rolled toward the water. One of the front caster wheels slid off the bank, and Brian and the chair tumbled into the deepest part of the pond.

It all happened too fast for Brian to comprehend. With a large splash, he landed face-first in the water. He had just enough time for one gulp of air before he and the wheelchair sank.

He thrashed the best he could but only succeeded in separating himself from the chair, which promptly plunged to the bottom of the pond. Brian panicked. "All I can do is hold my breath and hope someone saves me," he thought.

Then he caught a glimpse of something rising rapidly from below. It was round and had bright colors of red and yellow and blue. As it got closer, he realized it was a beach ball. And when he saw dark hair waving alongside of it, he thought it might be Cassie. Elation filled him as he squinted though the sun-streaked water. He watched as Cassie, who was hugging the ball, began to ascend toward the surface.

She was coming directly at him. Drawing nearer, she released the ball. It continued its rapid upward journey.

Suddenly they were nose to nose, and everything felt right. Her smile was so big that a bubble escaped from her gleaming teeth and headed to the surface. She held him under his arms and kicked hard. Together they made their way to air and sunshine and life.

When their heads emerged, Cassie gasped for air, and Brian caught a lung full of water. He began to cough and choke. Then he noticed Tommy preparing to dive in.

Cassie held onto Brian and swam toward the bank. Tommy knelt on the shore and reached to grab onto Brian's shirt. All the while, Cassie hugged Brian and kissed his face.

"I missed you," she said tenderly. "Do you know how much?"

"Yeah," Brian said between gasping coughs.

"Will you please let go of him?" Tommy spat. "I can't pull you both out at the same time!"

She released her stranglehold on Brian. Finally, Tommy was able to drag Brian's weak body onto the bank.

"I feel sick," Brian said.

Mom rolled him onto his side, and he vomited warm pond water again and again. He was nauseous, dizzy, and exhausted. With great effort, he managed to get himself up on all fours and then he puked again, while Cassie rubbed his back and assured him that he'd be okay.

At that moment, when he was at one of the all-time worst moments of his life, he realized the depth of Cassie's love for him. "I am puking my guts out and this crazy girl is rubbing my back," he thought.

The vomiting eventually subsided, and he managed to sit back and support himself with his arms. He wiped his face with the back of his hand and looked her in the eyes. She knelt in front of him on the wet grass, and Brian felt like she was gazing right into his soul.

"You're back! I'm so glad you made it back!" she sang.

"Likewise," Brian said between coughs. "Hey! Are you hurt? What happened down there?"

Cassie's white blouse and shorts stuck to her. She had some of his puke on her shirt, and her hair was wild with random strands clinging to her neck and cheeks. The reflecting sun played off the side of her face making her look like some kind of glossy angel.

"You are the most beautiful thing I have ever seen," said Brian, and at that moment he meant it with all his heart.

Mom leaned against a dangling willow tree and put one arm around Tommy's shoulder as they looked on.

Cassie shivered a moment and goose bumps rose on her arms. She took a breath, and pushed her hair back out of her eyes. "I got in the little boat and used a rock to take me to the bottom, and it worked! I found the beach ball in the garage."

"How in the world did you get a beach ball down there?" Brian asked.

"I brought it down deflated, and then blew it up when I was in the tunnel."

"Genius."

"My plan was to find the crystal on the bottom of the pond and use it to open the membrane. There was no sign of it, at first, but I did find the hole in the bottom of the pond and I went into the tunnel. I had your rubber flashlight with me, and when I waved it around, I saw a little sparkle where the crystal must have dropped. So I picked it up. It was mostly covered in moss."

She took the crystal from her pocket and held it in her hand. "I rubbed the moss off, like this." She moved her hands as if she were polishing an apple. "And the crystal came clean.

I guessed that it must have rotated when it fell through the hole and closed the membrane. Then I remembered how you turned it when you opened the membrane. It was like you were turning a doorknob. So that's what I was going to do. I was going to open the membrane and go look for you."

"Go on," said Brian "Then what happened?"

"I heard some gurgling and looked up. The cloud was coming down through the hole and into the tunnel. I hid under a big root and stayed really still. The cloud has grown huge! I watched it move through the tunnel and right up to the membrane. It touched the little cloud that was still caught in the membrane and made little squeaky noises, like it was trying to communicate. It seemed to be talking through the part of the cloud that was trapped in the membrane."

"Like when you put a string between two cans," Brian interjected. "Weren't you scared?"

"Yeah, I was scared!" Cassie looked down. "And that is when I lost my nerve. I just wanted to get out of there. I know you think I am a toughie and all, but maybe you're wrong. I was trapped down there with that disgusting blob all night. I kept thinking what it was like when you and I got swallowed up in that guck, and I didn't want that to happen again. When the cloud finally left, I didn't go through the membrane to look for you. I started to think that the other part of the cloud was waiting for me on the other side. That's when I lost my nerve."

Brian noticed a small tremor in her voice. "It's okay," he said. "Maybe the cloud was waiting for you on the other side. It's normal to be afraid. It's even smart. You're very lucky it didn't smell you. It must have had a one-track mind. And I still think you are the strongest person I have ever met."

"The cloud! Where did it go?" said Cassie.

"It shot out of the pond and headed to who knows

where," Tommy said.

"Don't worry. We'll find out where it went," Brian assured her.

Cassie embraced him, squeezing tightly. As she pulled away, she did a double-take. She fingered some of the hair on the left side of his bangs. "Brian, you have some green hair."

"What? That's weird. My body has been neglected but I don't know why it would turn my hair green. I'm afraid my body is wrecked."

"I will help you," said Cassie. "I will make some yellow fluid tonight for you to soak in."

She turned to Tommy. "I need you to help me find about seventy yellow smocken berries, the little kind without the thorns. And I'll need five cups of blue leaf oil and several bags of ripe turnips."

"We don't have any of those things here—well, except for the turnips," Tommy said.

"That just will not get it done. The turnips are the least important part. They are mostly for looks. They bob around so nicely in the tub."

"Oh, and by the way," Brian began, trying to sound casual, "remember our nemesis—the big bad evil one. You know—Leether? I did it! I beat him. He will never sacrifice anyone ever again."

A look of complete shock washed across Cassie's face in a tidal wave of disbelief. Her eyes widened, and a smile stretched across her face like an inflating balloon. "Leether's dead? Really? How in the world did you do that? It was your aura, wasn't it? He couldn't stop you. Wow, I never thought it would work. I mean I hoped it would, but I don't know. It is truly amazing news. I am so proud of you! How did you kill him? Did you…"

"Whoa! Take a breath. Okay, technically he is alive, but

it's a life worse than death. And the specters who took him will have him dead soon enough. And no, it wasn't my aura that got him. I was inside a beast—and your m—"

Brian stopped right there, his mind racing. He thought, "If Cassie knows her mom is alive she will want to go back, even if it means going into the tunnel again. I have to think about this. Maybe it's best if she doesn't know."

He said, "Um, I mean m—man it was great, and I wish you could have seen the look on his face."

"That is just amazing! I am so relieved and shocked at the same time." She clapped her hands together. "I want to hear every detail."

"When we get home we'll have a lot of stories to swap. And I guess I'll have to settle for a plain hot water bath," said Brian.

He frowned, as he began thinking, "Why would she want to stay here with someone like me who can hardly move, when she'd have the power to go back home and be with her mom?" At that moment he decided not to tell her, and at once felt both guilty and selfish.

Cassie knelt beside him and brushed the wet curly hair out of his eyes. "What is it now? You suddenly look so sad. What's wrong?"

"Nothing," he lied. "I'm just thinking about the bad shape my body is in."

Cassie moved closer, and when she did, the morning sunshine illuminated Brian's face. "Something's different with your eyes, too," she said.

"What do you mean?"

"Well when the sun hits them, your pupils turn into little slits, like the eyes of a lizard."

"Let me see," said Tommy.

"They do?" said Brian. "Are you joking with me?" Then

he thought about it a moment. "Oh, no, that's like the beast's eyes! I wonder if I have some residual effect from being inside that beast for too long. Maybe a little of the beast's aura mixed with part of mine when I left its body behind."

"How did you get inside a beast?" she asked, bewildered.

"My aura got locked into it."

Tommy pushed Cassie aside to get a better look. "Whoa, Bri, your eyes are freaky."

"I can't wait to hear that story," Cassie said, wrinkling her nose. "If your aura's got a little beast mixed in it, eventually it may show up physically. Like when a bee moves pollen from one flower to another."

"You mean like cross-pollination? Are you sure it works that way with auras?"

Cassie shrugged. "Maybe."

"Okay, I'll keep an eye out for any outward beastliness. Geeze, I hope I don't get any uglier."

Mom rubbed Brian's back and hugged him from behind. "Don't worry. You are still a beautiful kid. It's so overwhelming, isn't it? I love you all. I have you back and that is all that stands between me and a mental institution."

"The lizard eyes are so cool! Do they work well in the dark?" Tommy asked.

"I don't know."

"I bet they do. Can we check them out tonight?"

"What I want most is to hang on to who I am," Brian said with frustration.

"It's okay," said Cassie. "We are always changing. Don't fight it. Each event in life will make us a little different; the trick is to keep your core clean—clean and hard like a perfectly smooth stone. If your core is strong, you may change on the outside but never on the inside."

Tommy laughed. "What the heck does that mean? You

sound like Ebil."

Brian smiled warmly. He leaned forward and touched his forehead to Cassie's.

"The wheelchair is on the bottom of the pond," said Tommy. "I'd better piggyback ride you home."

"Can you carry me?"

"Yeah, I think so. You aren't so heavy anymore." Tommy lifted Brian's arm and hoisted him over his shoulders like a bag of oats.

Brian slid down his brother's back. It was uncomfortable, but he hung on as Tommy began carrying him up the path toward the house.

A stiff breeze kicked up, and a small dust devil spun on the path in front of them, stopping them in their tracks. "Follow the three-legged rabbit," said a breathy voice.

"Huh?" said Brian. "Eurus, is that you? Hey, you're already back to talking in the wind."

"Three-legged rabbit?" said Cassie.

"This isn't helping, Eurus. What are you trying to tell me?" Brian asked. "How do we protect everyone from the cloud? Is there a good way to kill it?"

The wind spun and expanded wider. As it dissipated, the voice said, "Miracle Mix." Brian frowned. "Wow, that was the most confusing thing Eurus has ever said. Maybe he's losing it. Now he's part specter and part...whatever it is he used to be."

Tommy laughed. "Well said, Brian."

# CHAPTER TWELVE
# MIRACLE MIX

THE NEXT day, Mom took Brian to see the family doctor. When they returned home, Tommy and Cassie were anxiously waiting for them at the kitchen table.

Mom pulled open the screen door with a creak and then kicked it all the way open with the side of her foot. She pushed a borrowed wheelchair in with one smooth movement before the door banged shut behind her.

"Well, what did the doctor say?" Tommy asked.

Brian furrowed his brow and burst out with the bad news. "He said I have the atrophy of a bed-ridden, ninety-year-old man."

"It's so severe the doctor was mystified," said Mom. "He said that just lying in bed for a week would not have made it that bad."

Brian scowled, "I wanted to tell him, 'Well, what about if your body was petrified for a week with it's life force sucked out of it—would that make it worse?'"

"The prognosis is very grim," Mom said with a frown. "The doctor said Brian might never walk again without support. He's scheduled for physical therapy three times a week, and they strongly suggested we buy some machine that we can't afford in order to move his legs and arms, and loosen them up."

• • •

Despite the discouraging prognosis, Brian began feeling stronger by the time evening came around. His arms did start to loosen up, and he was able to roll the wheelchair without assistance.

Mom had invited Grandma Rae to have a spaghetti dinner with them. She arrived with several glistening jars of red sauce packed neatly in a stylish wicker basket that was draped with a red-checkered cloth.

"You can just put the sauce on the counter," Brian said as she stepped around his wheelchair and into the kitchen.

"Hi, Grandma," Cassie said cheerfully.

"It seems like she just loves to say grandma out loud," Brian thought.

Tommy entered the room and the fine basket immediately caught his gaze. "When did Red Riding Hood get here?" he asked.

Grandma Rae chuckled. "It's my basket, silly. You know, I so enjoy being around you kids. Well, except for that story you told me about how a tentacle grabbed Cassie and pulled her into the mud. That scared me almost to death," she said, putting her hand over her heart.

Cassie sighed. "Yeah, sorry about the red blob story. I just wanted you to understand everything."

Grandma Rae nodded. "I've been meaning to tell you that some of my neighbor's kittens, two chickens, and a pig disappeared last week. Most neighbors suspect poachers, but poachers don't have any interest in kittens. I have been putting two and two together, and I fear that devilish cloud of yours has gobbled them up. You kids are going to get killed if you aren't more careful. Is that the kind of creature my Sarah had to contend with in the other world?"

Brian cleared his throat. "Yeah, but I think she will be okay now."

Cassie grabbed a hold of the push handles and spun Brian's wheelchair so he'd face her. "What did you say? She'll be okay now? But how would you know that?" She sat across from Brian and connected with him at eye level. "My mother is dead."

Brian panicked and began thinking fast. "I can't look either of them in the eye and ever lie to them. If they ask the right questions, it's over…I have to tell them."

He rubbed his forehead with the side of his hand to stall, as he tried to put together his answer. But he drew a blank. He studied Grandma Rae's and Cassie's expressions. They were staring at him intently. The long pause grew uncomfortable, and by their expressions he could tell they knew something was wrong.

"Well, uh…I heard some things," Brian said.

"What did you hear? You heard some things about my mom?" Cassie put her hand on Brian's knee.

"It wasn't anything I heard," he began. He took a deep breath, and the words spilled from his mouth. "I actually met her. It's a long story…"

"You met her? Then she's still alive, right?" Cassie was nearly shrieking.

Grandma Rae gasped and covered her mouth with one hand while she grasped Brian's wrist with the other. "Tell us," she said.

"Yes, she's alive," Brian said. "The whole story about her dying in childbirth was a lie. Leether sent her over the mountain after you were born. He told her that if she ever came back she would be sacrificed."

"Why are you just telling me this now?" Cassie demanded. She pulled her hand away and stood. Folding her arms angrily, she snarled, "I never ever thought, even for a moment, that you would keep secrets from me."

"Well, I thought you would want to go back."

"Brian Hummel, you'd better come out with all of it, right now, and I mean every dark detail no matter how disturbing. Do you understand?"

"What happened to my baby?" asked Grandma Rae. "I want to know. I just want the truth."

Brian paused to collect his thoughts. He took a deep breath, and said, "I spent most of my time in the other world with her. She is kind of banged up, but should recover. She has friends who will stand with her if things get bad."

He squirmed in his chair, and then continued. "I can see a lot of her in both of you. She is smart and clever, and I like her. But I was afraid to tell you two about her when I saw that Cassie had the crystal. I just thought Cassie would leave to go back for her the first chance she got. I guess I was being selfish."

"You were wrong for not telling me," said Cassie. "And it was selfish of you!" She stood quietly for a moment shaking her head. Then she clenched her teeth, turned away, and stomped out of the room. Everyone froze until they heard her bedroom door slam.

"Not exactly the reaction I was expecting," said Brian.

During the entire exchange, Grandma Rae had been listening quietly with her mouth open. She smiled, stepped toward Brian and hugged him. "You have just lifted a heavy black cloud from me and eased a lifetime of pain. I feel light as a butterfly!" She tilted back her gray head and raised her hands in the air. "My Sarah lives!" she yelled, squeezing her frail hands into tight little fists. Her wrinkled face beamed and warmed her teary eyes.

"Wow, two different women and two different reactions," said Brian.

Tommy pulled up a chair and plopped down at the table. "I was thinking that if we can find out where the cloud hides, we can kill it with a big fireball." He flicked his fingertips as if flames were shooting from them.

"Maybe we could use a flamethrower or a blowtorch," Brian interjected.

"We don't own a flamethrower, and I don't think they sell them at the hardware store either," Mom said.

Brian nearly jumped at the sound of his mom's voice. "How long have you been standing there in the hallway?"

"I heard the screen door when Rae came in, but don't worry, I have only been eavesdropping for a few moments. Do you know how crazy your conversation just sounded? Killing an evil cloud of goo with a flamethrower?"

Tommy gave her a blank stare. "I thought he had a good idea."

Then Brian whispered to Tommy, "I've got to oil that hinge."

Tommy giggled.

Mom frowned, as if she assumed the joke was on her. Then her eyes narrowed. "We are still a family here and you have to start keeping me in the loop. I've given up being able to control the situation. I can't even begin to know what's going on, so how can I control anything? I just hope and pray we all live through it. I want to protect you and help you, but I just don't know how. What do I do?"

"This is all very surreal to me, too," said Brian. "But we're not little kids anymore. Just protect yourself, and we will take care of our end."

"You don't understand," she said. "I will always be your mother. I will always want to protect you and make things right for you. It doesn't matter how old you get, I will always feel that way."

Grandma Rae moved over and gave mom a warm embrace. They began to cry. After a few moments Rae, broke away and wiped her damp eyes. Then she lifted a gleaming red jar of spaghetti sauce from the basket and held it up with pride.

"You brought lots of sauce," said Brian.

"I call it Grandma Rae's Miracle Mix."

Brian froze. "You call it Miracle Mix?"

"Yes. Have you heard of it? I sell it at farmers markets and bake sales. I brought several over for you. It has two secret ingredients that prevent anyone from copying my recipe."

"I haven't heard of it. But I must say it would have to be tasty, since you gave it such a special name and show it with such pride," said Mom.

Looking bewildered, Brian began thinking out loud. "When Eurus spoke to us in the wind he said two things: Follow the three-legged rabbit, and Miracle Mix. Does Eurus think we can beat the cloud using spaghetti sauce? He has lost his mind."

"Oh no, Brian," said Grandma Rae. "It is for eating, and I never give out the recipe either. That would be like a magician telling how he does his trick."

"Well, have you ever used Worcestershire sauce?" Mom asked. "That's what my mother always said gave her sauce its special kick."

Rae nodded, and then there was an awkward pause in the conversation. Rae could have filled the void by talking about what was in her sauce, but she chose to remain silent.

She poured a full jar of sauce into a large saucepan. Soon the kitchen was abuzz with bubbling sauce and clanging plates. A kitchen that normally smelled of lemon-scented cleaning products was now thick with the fragrance of an Italian restaurant.

Mom parted the curtains over the kitchen sink. "It's getting dark already. Summer is almost over."

Brian laughed. "I can just see it now. We get back to our first day at school and they ask us what we did on our summer vacation."

Meanwhile, Rae stirred her sauce. She chatted with Brian's mom about the importance of a good sauce recipe.

"Cassie!" Mom called out. "Now why isn't that girl coming to dinner?"

The meal was served on a steaming platter. Brian's face lit up as he smelled the rich aroma, and he rolled up to his spot at the table.

Mom began to cut the meatballs into small pieces for Brian.

"You never have been much of a meat-eater," she said.

His eyes slid back in his head with pleasure as the juice rolled across his tongue. "I can take it from here, Mom," he said. "I am strong enough to stab it and get it into my own mouth."

"Cassie!" he yelled toward the hallway. "Come on. I'm really sorry. Just come and eat."

Mom nodded. "It surprises me you wanted meat so badly."

"I know! I never much liked hamburger before because you always cooked it too rare. It would sit on my plate in a disgusting pool of blood that you call juice, which somehow made it even more disgusting. But I gotta say, right now I hunger for meat like an addict. I bet I could eat this stuff raw with blood dripping from my mouth and like it."

"Brian, you're scaring me," said Mom.

"This meat is like pouring gas into an empty tank. I can feel it tingling all through my arms and down into my toes. Eating meat never did that to me before."

"Are you okay?"

"Very okay," Brian said, with a huge smile. "I feel better with each swallow."

"Your body must be starved for protein," said Mom.

"I have the beast's hunger," said Brian. "Maybe I will heal like a beast, too. It reminds me of something Ebil told me at the Pit of Despair."

"Was it a rhyme?" said Tommy.

"Cassie! Time for dinner!" Mom yelled again.

"She is really pissed at me, Mom. Please, don't call her again. I think we need to let her cool off for a while."

Mom gave Brian a quizzical look.

"The rhyme?" Tommy asked impatiently.

"Oh yeah, I can't remember the first part—something about everything stacks up and every smooth thing cracks up. But I do remember the last line. It was, 'Every experience makes changes, and your outer-self rearranges.'"

Brian detected a quiet squeak, barely heard over the dinner conversation. He looked up from his plate. "Who left the door open?" He was startled by red ooze pushing open the screen door and seeping into the breezeway.

"AHHHH!" he yelled. He instinctively shoved his wheelchair away from the approaching blob. "Run! Run! Get out of here!" he screamed.

Tommy was standing at the counter. He dropped his glass of juice and sent it crashing to the floor.

Brian rolled back to the table and snatched up a large knife from the cutting board. Mom and Grandma Rae first reacted to the crashing glass, and then turned and saw the blob pressing its way into the room. Stunned, they jerked away from the cloud and fell out of their chairs.

When a gooey red tentacle stretched out of the blob and reached for Brian, he spun and hacked off the tip of it with the knife. The blob of red goo slapped against the wooden floor.

Grandma Rae pulled herself to her feet and went for the pan of sauce on the stove. Trembling, she grasped the handle and flung the hot sauce at the enormous blob.

The sauce burned into the cloud like hot water on cold snow. The blob sizzled and snapped. It lurched backward, and in an instant had retreated through the door.

To Brian's surprise, Grandma Rae still was not done. In heroic fashion, she followed it out the door screaming, "Shoo! Shoo!"

"Grandma Rae, get back here!" Brian pleaded. He dropped the bloody knife in his lap and rolled quickly after her.

Tommy had the same idea, and they both collided in the doorway as they left the kitchen. Tommy tumbled over Brian and the chair. They all went crashing violently to the floor. Brian suddenly realized that Tommy was now pinned under both himself and the toppled chair. Tommy tugged and squirmed. Brian was of little help. Finally, Tommy kicked himself free. Pushing himself up, he ran out the door after Grandma Rae.

"Come back!" Tommy called out in desperation.

Brian watched as Cassie ran into the room. He couldn't move; he was still on his side in the breezeway—one wheel of his chair still spinning.

Spaghetti sauce had splattered across the kitchen floor and cupboards. Struggling to her feet, Mom yelled,

"What's happening?"

"Rae ran after the cloud!" Brian hollered. He used his arms to crawl army-style to the backdoor and began to push it open with his palm.

Cassie pushed it the rest of the way open. She stepped over Brian and ran into the dusty yard.

Brian scanned the yard but didn't see the cloud. With his torso halfway through the doorway he rolled onto his side and looked up. He was able to catch a glimpse of the last remnants of the cloud as it rose and disappeared over the house.

"Grandma Rae!" Cassie called out. She turned to face Tommy. "What is going on? Did the cloud get her?"

"I don't know," said Tommy. "When I came through the door, the cloud was retreating, and Grandma Rae was gone."

"Get in the house," Mom screamed. "Get inside before it comes back. Get in the house NOW! Lock all the doors and windows."

Mom grabbed onto Brian's ankles and dragged him back inside. "This thing has figured out where we live," she moaned.

Cassie and Tommy entered the house, and Tommy slammed and locked the door behind them.

Cassie's face was contorted in rage and grief. Her body shook and her eyes were wide with terror. "It's got her," she screamed. "I can't believe I just lost my grandmother. She's gone, and it will be coming after the rest of us next."

"Poor Grandma Rae," Mom sobbed.

"I know we're all shocked and upset, but we have got to clear our heads and think," Brian said, still lying on the floor.

Mom looked at Brian, confused. "Clear our heads? Rae was killed, and you expect me to clear my head?"

"I have learned to concentrate when things are going

bad. We can all freak out later but right now…well, right now we have to think."

"What's that smell? It smells like old socks and tuna in here," said Tommy.

"The sauce ate through the blob. I think we smell burned-up cloud in here," said Brian.

Tommy pointed at a piece of blob on the floor. "It's still moving."

"Quick, get it in a jar," said Brian. "We can use it."

Tommy took an empty glass canning jar from the cupboard and scooped the red blob inside, using the lid.

"Seal it tightly," said Cassie, as she retrieved the bloody knife from the floor. "The cloud was full of blood. That means it has eaten recently."

"G-get rid of it," Mom stammered. Without saying another word, she grabbed a broom and began sweeping up the broken glass.

Brian pulled himself to a sitting position. "No! We keep it. It can be used to make us invisible to the cloud."

"Where did you learn that?" asked Tommy. He set the jar on the kitchen table.

"Cassie's mom taught me. The cloud is able to see by using its sense of smell. If we boil this piece of cloud and neutralize the poison, we can smear it on ourselves. Basically, the cloud can't smell its own stink."

Brian watched the red blob in the jar start to move a little. "Look," he said, tapping on the jar. "It's recovering from the shock of being cut off. It's trying to become its own little cloud now."

"Seriously, do we have to have this thing in the middle of the kitchen table?" asked Mom.

Tommy wiped some splattered sauce off the cupboard with his finger and lifted it toward the jar. "Want some sauce?" he teased.

The blob slammed against the opposite side of the jar, tipping it over. The jar rolled across the table and into Mom's waiting hands.

"That is enough!" yelled Mom. "If that jar had broken, we would have a mini-terror infecting our house. I'm going to take care of it right now! I'll flush it down the toilet!"

Brian shook his head. "I know that works well for dead goldfish and spiders, but do you want that thing coming up while you're…"

"Enough! I get it."

"Don't worry. Heat or some ingredient in Rae's spaghetti sauce will kill it."

Cassie filled a pan with hot water. She put it on the stove, and within minutes, the water reached the boiling point. Using tongs, she carefully placed the jar into the bubbling water.

Meanwhile Brian let Tommy help him back into his now-righted chair. Even though Cassie wasn't talking to him yet, Brian was relieved that she hadn't gone back to her room.

Wearing an oven mitt, Cassie loosened the lid of the jar, after she was sure the glob was dead.

"You're stinking up the whole house," said Mom.

"She has to release the pressure on the jar," Brian said, trying to show support.

Cassie nodded and put the lid back on.

"Believe me," said Brian. "The stench is a worthwhile trade-off. Now that the cloud knows where we live, the rules are that anytime we go outside we put on a little bit of this boiled cloud goo, and it will mask our scent with its own."

Brian gazed at Cassie with big eyes. "I'm so sorry, Cassie. Are we okay?"

She frowned, but somewhere in her eyes, Brian saw a glimmer of hope.

"Look, I'm glad you don't want me to leave, because I want to stay," she said. "There is no other place in any world that I would rather be. But don't think that gets you off the hook."

Brian nodded. "From now on, I will always be straight with you. You can trust me—honest."

"Okay," said Cassie. "Knowing that my mom is alive is enough for me right now. I have never met her. I don't know her so I can't miss her the same way I will miss Grandma Rae."

"Okay," said Brian.

"Nonetheless, I do want to hear all about her."

"I will tell you everything I know."

"Understand, I want the truth, always—no matter how hard it might be to say it. Never give me a false reality. Truth is reality, and reality is truth."

• • •

That night Brian got in bed without any assistance. He pulled up his covers snugly under his chin. Then he sighed deeply and closed his eyes, exhausted from the day.

Cassie sat by his bedside and verbally relived the incident that cost poor Grandma Rae her life. Brian found the ache and pain of the loss emotionally and physically draining. He listened to Cassie's voice until he could no longer keep his eyes open.

Deep into the night, Brian dreamt he was back in the beast somewhere below the swamp. He looked around at the damp steamy maze of caverns and dripping water. He felt a piercing sharp pain to his temple. A slippery specter was smiling at him, while drawing his blood. He swung his arm franticly to knock off the suction-cupped finger.

The pain jerked him awake. He reached up and rubbed the side of his head.

"Wait! I moved my arm and it didn't hurt!"

To his amazement, he was on his feet and standing next to his bed. "Great," he said sarcastically "I'm sleepwalking again. But hey, I'm standing! Not bad for a guy the doctor said would never walk again. It hasn't even been a day."

He took a careful, measured step and, although his knees ached, he didn't fall. So he took another. He continued to walk, all the while running one hand along the wall to steady himself, until he reached the bathroom door.

Flicking on the light, he thrust his face just inches from the mirror. "Now let me get a look at you," he said to himself.

At first, he was startled by the pale, gaunt face of his reflection. "I must have lost fifteen pounds!"

His hair had a thin streak of dark green that sprang from the left side of his bangs. "My eyes look okay. Oh yeah, they said it was when the sun hit them."

He glanced at the light above the mirror, and his big pupils shrank into lizard-like slits. "Wow, everything does stack up."

He turned out the light and moved back toward his room. "It's getting light out already. It must be early morning." As he entered the room he noticed the time: 1:11 am. "It's not that it's getting lighter, it's my beast eyes. Dark will never look as dark again."

• • •

The next morning Brian stunned his mother by staggering to the breakfast table under his own power. "Brian!" said

Mom "Oh, my word! You can walk." She ran to help him to the table, but he waved her off.

Brian pulled out a chair and plopped down. "Can we bypass the physical therapy bit? They don't know what they are talking about."

"Perhaps they've never had a patient like you before."

Brian laughed. "Ya think? Can we eat? I have never been so hungry in all my life!" Mom put a big bowl of cereal in front of him. He could hardly wait for a spoon to dig in. She followed up with a plate full of crackling bacon right out of the skillet and fluffy yellow scrambled eggs.

"Wow," said Tommy. "You look way better."

Brian beamed. A small puff of scrambled egg dropped from his lip. "I'm getting stronger by the hour. They said I wouldn't walk again, and in less than a day I don't need the wheelchair—or even a walker."

Cassie staggered in wearing light-blue, button-down pajamas. Her disheveled hair looked fluffy. She yawned as she wiped the sleep from her eyes.

"How do you look so good first thing in the morning?" Brian said.

"Brian!" Mom admonished. "Will you stop flirting with the girl?"

Cassie gazed warmly at Brian and said, "You look so much more alive today."

Cassie filled a plate with scrambled eggs and bacon, and then poured herself some orange juice. She slid her hand along Brian's neck as she sat down. "It's time we talk. We have a big problem. The little cloud is not so little anymore. It took Grandma. You saw the size of it. It must hide during the day and hunt at night."

Tommy piped up, "It's got to be hiding somewhere good because no one has seen it or talked about it."

"It's just a matter of time before it starts taking more people. This is like some scary horror movie, only this stuff is real," said Brian. "This is actually a bigger threat than Leether ever was. This thing is going to eat and grow until our world is just as messed up as the other one. It's like a virus. It has to be stopped right now, before it spreads."

Cassie nodded in agreement. "The cloud doesn't think like you or me. It uses accumulated brainpower. It needs both Leether's brain and its own brain to be fully functional. Leether was its host. You could even say that he was the cloud master. I am more positive than ever that the cloud in this world was communicating with Leether through the cloud caught in the membrane."

"If that is true, then I must have broken off communication when I put Leether away."

"The cloud can't be too happy about that," said Cassie. "It probably waited at the membrane all night, and when news from Leether never came it blasted off confused and angry."

"It's an angry, eating demon with half a brain. Who knows what it will do next. How do we warn everyone? If we breathe even a word of it they will just be more convinced we are all crazy."

"I have lived in fear of the cloud all my life and now, for the first time, I feel like I have the power to do something about it," Cassie said. She stared intensely at Brian and tightened up her fist. "I want to beat it," she snarled.

He stretched and twisted his head to the side. With a loud crack, a few stiffened vertebrae fell back into place. "I'm in, but how do we beat it?" he asked.

# CHAPTER THIRTEEN
# THE RABBIT'S PAW

"Over here!" Tommy yelled from across the backyard.

Brian unscrewed the jar of goo and dabbed a little cloud stink on his neck. Then he headed out the backdoor.

"I found something behind the barn," Tommy called.

Just past the tractor, Brian spotted his brother kneeling over something. The something was obscured by the barn's shadow.

Tommy lifted a silver object he'd pulled from the dandelions and held it over his head by the handle. "Look what I found—a saucepan!"

Brian slowed from a labored run to a walk, and came alongside Tommy. He accepted the pan from his brother and examined it closely, wiping the inside with his thumb. "This is the pan Rae was swinging at the cloud. It has dried sauce inside."

He glanced back toward the house. "This doesn't make sense to me. I saw the cloud float over the house and head in the opposite direction. If the cloud got her, then how did the pan get way over here?"

"Someone or something could have dragged her over

here," Tommy suggested. "Whoever or whatever would have had time to do it while we were tripping over each other in the doorway. If you think about it, the cloud was trying to get away from Grandma Rae and her sauce."

Brian knelt and began searching among the weeds. "Hey! What's this? A rabbit's foot?" he said. He picked it up and began brushing off the black ants that were scurrying around on it.

"It's kind of gross," said Tommy. Blood had crusted on the bottom where it had been cut off. "It isn't cool, like the ones at the drugstore. This one has dull brown fur; the ones at the store are dyed pink or blue and have a nice gold chain attached to them. I guess I never thought about the rabbit that used to be on the other end of it."

Brian stood and held it up to Tommy's face. "Where there's a rabbit's foot, it's only logical to assume that somewhere there is a very irritated three-legged bunny limping around."

"The rabbit must be dead already if we have its foot," Tommy said. He reached out and rubbed the soft top of the foot with his index finger. "These things are supposed to be lucky."

"Not for the rabbit," said Brian. "And the rabbit would have to be alive in order to lead us anywhere. Remember what Eurus said: 'Follow the three-legged rabbit.' So, if we can find the rabbit, where will it lead us? To Rae or whatever took her? To the cloud's hiding place? Or both? Whoever cut off the rabbit's foot would probably know where to find the rest of the rabbit."

"So, who would be cruel enough to cut the leg off a bunny and leave it to limp around?"

Tommy thought a moment. "Joey and Roger are the only kids sick enough to do something like that."

"Okay then, let's go knock on their doors and find out

what they know," said Brian.

"Those guys will be playing softball this afternoon at the old field. Let's go over like we're going to play. Then we can ask those two jerks what they know about this foot."

"Wow! I forgot about our Monday softball games. Life has been so upside down, I don't have the same routine anymore. I'm feeling pretty good, but not steady enough to run hard yet."

"Just take a few warm-up swings. We'll ask around about the foot and then go," said Tommy.

Brian nodded. "That works."

Brian heard a noise behind him. He whirled around to see Cassie kicking up a dandelion as she walked toward them.

"What are you doing?" she asked. "What's softball?"

"It is a game with a bat and ball. You hit the ball with the bat and run around the bases."

"You hit a bat with a ball?" she said, scrunching her nose.

"Do you know what a bat and ball is?"

"Sure," she said.

Brian grinned. "You should come with us to see what we're talking about. It might be a different kind of bat than the one you're thinking of. And guess what? We found Rae's pan and a rabbit's foot." He showed her both objects.

"Really? What do you think that means?"

"It means something doesn't add up. We're going over to the ball field to dig up some answers."

"Okay, but we have got to take precautions. I am bringing a jar of Grandma Rae's sauce with us. And we should put a little cloud goo behind each ear just in case the cloud changes its routine and comes out during the day."

"Brian, you've got to do something about your eyes," said Tommy. "I'm getting used to them, but the guys might freak out if they see them in the bright sun."

"Already thought of that. I'll just wear sunglasses on sunny days. No big deal. It'll be all right."

Brian knelt to retie his loose shoelaces. He noticed, as he pulled up hard on the laces, that the feathery weakness he had felt just days earlier was being replaced with solid muscle. "I feel better," he thought. "Maybe the things I took from the beast are a blessing and not a curse."

"Let's head inside and get our softball mitts," he said.

• • •

When they arrived at the field, Brian noted that some of the guys were already warming up. It was a rag tag field on the edge of town. Rusty fences in disrepair surrounded it. An overgrown wooded area pressed against the outfield fences as if trying to get in, and dust kicked up in the infield with the slightest breeze.

"Just have a seat on the bench," Brian said to Cassie. "I'll answer your questions while you watch us play."

Cassie smiled and squirmed with anticipation. She looked thrilled to see all these interesting people interacting in her new world. Her new tan shorts, matching sandals, and a cream-colored blouse—all bought last week by Brian's mom—gave her a very stunning appearance.

Brian couldn't help but stare as she brushed her glistening hair away from her face. She emanated such cuteness that Brian couldn't help himself. He touched her gently on the cheek. "Your freckles are coming out."

"Freckles?" She brought her hand up to her cheek and tried to rub them off.

"Don't worry, they look cute."

Brian finally pried his eyes off Cassie and pushed his hand into the dry, leather softball mitt. Once supple and soft, the mitt had become cracked and stiff. It was then that he realized how long it had been since he had spent time with his friends.

Brian noticed that Toby's and Dave's eyes were fixed on Cassie—the new girl—with the black shiny hair. They smiled and walked forward to greet her.

"Hi there," Toby said with a grin.

Cassie nodded in his direction but didn't return his stare.

Getting little reaction, Toby walked over to Brian, who was by the fence pounding his mitt with his fist. "That your girlfriend?"

"Yeah—she is."

"She's hot," he said under his breath.

"Smoking," agreed Dave. Moving closer to Brian, he said, "How did you pull that one off? I never saw her before. Did she just move here from Hot Girl Land or something? And hey, Brian, aren't you supposed to be paralyzed?"

"Coma…I was in a coma…sort of."

"How do you sort of get in a coma?"

"The same way you sort of get out of it," Brian said, as he practiced catching the ball. "I have something to ask you guys, and it's important. Have you ever seen this?" he dug in his jeans pocket and pulled out the bloody little foot.

"Not exactly," said Dave, as he inspected it.

"What does not exactly mean?"

"Well, I've never seen it before, but this reminds me of the kind of animal torture thing Joey would be into."

"That's what we were thinking. Is he playing today?"

"He's never missed a game, but I would have to say he probably won't show. Haven't you heard? He ran off. No one has seen him for days."

Brian scowled and leaned against the rusty fence to whisper in Tommy's ear. "Let's play a while, and if Joey is a no-show it means that evil cloud probably got him, too."

"I bet he tasted bitter," said Tommy.

"Not funny, Tom. It's a kid's life we are talking about—whether we like him or not."

"What did you say?" Dave asked. "Not funny? Right, it's not funny. The cops have been looking for him. The neighbors are calling around to form a search party, too. Something bad could have happened."

"Look! Roger is already hitting on your lady," Toby said and then laughed.

Brian spun on his heel to see Roger in action. "Why did you invite him?"

"We needed the players."

Roger was stocky with hair black as ink. Despite his young age he had already sprouted several dark chest hairs, which he wore like a badge of "studliness." The sleeves of his black tee shirt were cut off and ragged.

"Does he even own any shirts with sleeves?" Dave asked.

"Give him a break," said Brian. "He's had to train his muscles to flex with every movement. It must take enormous concentration." He chuckled at his own joke.

On cue, Roger took off his shirt and handed it to Cassie. Then he glanced away for a moment, appearing to give her an opportunity to check out his impressive biceps.

Brian snarled at the shirtless Roger, who had placed one foot on the bench and was trying to engage Cassie in conversation. At first Brian felt a twinge of jealously, but then he quickly realized Cassie would rebuff him.

"Roger thinks he's a big stud," Brian said, as he did a mocking muscle magazine pose. "I have ten bucks says he either gets knocked on his butt or walks away scratching his head."

Just as the words left Brian's lips, Cassie swatted Roger's

hand off her knee. Then she stood and shoved his shirt into his chest.

Roger shook his head and picked up his mitt. He jogged over to Brian. "Hey! That girl says she's with you."

"That's right."

"Well, your girlfriend is weird!"

"Why? Because she doesn't like you?"

"No."

"Then there is another reason?"

"She's carrying around a glass jar, and when I asked her what it was and she said it was the Flower Witch's Miracle Mix."

"That's right. The Flower Witch is her grandma," said Brian.

"For real? My mom said the Flower Witch is probably the same sick-o who kidnapped Joey."

Dave stepped in. "No one knows if he was kidnapped. Look how long Brian and Tommy were gone, and they came back. Besides the Flower Witch is a made-up story."

"If it's made up, then who throws the stupid flowers in the pond?" Roger said.

"It's Cassie's grandma that throws the flowers in the pond," said Brian defensively. "But that does not make her a witch."

"It does when her granddaughter calls her one," Roger pointed out. "And your girlfriend—well, she smells funny. And when I say funny I mean a potent stink. She'd better find some new perfume. That smell stays with you even after you walk away. It's still burning my nose right now! It's kind of like dead carp mixed with gym locker room or something."

Brian pushed Roger away from him. "Shut up!"

Roger laughed. "Hey, she got some stink on you, too. I swear that is the same smell. Guys, you have got to check it out."

"Stop it," said Dave. "Who are you to talk about stink when your old man always smells like beer, cigars, and sweat?"

"Roger, shut up and warm up," said Brian.

"I'd like to play catch, but you idiots only brought one ball!"

Cassie looked on with interest. "Is this part of the game?" she called.

Brian shook his head and turned to his friends. "Look, obviously she's not from around here, so give her a break, okay? Her grandma is missing, too."

"Whatever," said Roger. "My old man might be a drunk, and he might be wrong about most things, but he's got one thing right. There's something funny going on at your farm."

With that, Roger walked backward and held up his mitt. "Hey stinky, throw me the ball."

Aggravated, Brian unintentionally threw the ball harder than necessary for the distance. Roger reacted in a defensive move and the ball went off the top of his mitt and careened off the fence. Then it ricocheted through the open gate and rolled to where Cassie sat.

She leaned forward, picked up the ball, and squeezed it with both hands. She stood and gave it a good shake next to her ear. Then she rapped it with her knuckles. "It doesn't feel so soft."

Several black birds fluttered to the chain link fence, just a few yards from her. She wound up and threw the ball hard at the birds. They lifted off in a flash but one of them flew into the ball's path. Its wing got clipped. It floundered for a moment and hit the ground. The bird flapped wildly in the dirt, and then righted itself and took off again.

The boys all stared in astonishment. "What is she doing?" Toby asked.

Brian looked at her confused. "Why did you do that?"

192

"Um, you said you hit the bat with the ball."

"No, it's hit the ball with the bat, and that wasn't even a bat. It was a black bird."

"Well, you said it was a different kind of bat, and that was the only black flying thing that I saw!" Somewhat frustrated she put her hands on her hips.

"It's okay. The bird recovered. No harm done—and good arm, by the way."

"Come on, Brian. Hit us a few fly balls while we wait for more players," Tommy said. Dave nodded, and he and Tommy trotted into the outfield, while Roger took a spot on the mound. Toby and Dan covered shortstop and third base.

"Try to get a hold of this one," said Roger. "It's my patented spinner-roo. All back spin and in on your wrist. You're in trouble cause dorks never hit it!"

The ball left Roger's hand and arced toward the plate. The threads of the ball were a blur as the ball spun rapidly. Brian zeroed in on it, his eyes reflecting the anger that suddenly welled inside his chest. He brought the bat back and growled, "GRAAAW!" With one enormous swing the ball cracked off the end of the bat unnaturally hard. It shot out of the field like it had been fired from a cannon.

The boys stood frozen in amazement. They watched, their mouths open wide, as the ball disappeared over the tops of the trees.

"What the heck was that?" Roger shouted.

Brian tried to slough it off. But after that hit, he knew things between him and his friends would never be the same.

"Game over. That ball will never be found," said Toby as he threw his mitt up in the air.

They all begin walking back toward the pitching mound.

"What a freak show," Roger snarled. But his tone reflected his uneasiness—as if he were covering his fears with a fierce bravado.

Roger pointed at Brian and demanded, "Who the heck are you? What have you done with Brian?"

Dan sniffed the air, when Tommy and Dave passed by him. "Tommy smells like dead fish, too," he said.

Roger scowled. "Did you rub on some secret Miracle Mix potion from the Flower Witch or something? Did you sell your soul to the devil? What is going on? No one—and I mean no one—hits a ball that far. It's just unnatural!"

"Why is it making you so angry?" asked Brian.

"It doesn't add up. You've never hit a ball out of the park before today. And now, all of a sudden you're Slamming Sammy Sosa or something. Time to come clean. Joey told me that he saw you turn into a ghost at the market, and I laughed at him. Now I don't know. I think it may have actually happened. Did you kidnap Joey and take him somewhere to shut him up? Oh, and what's with the sunglasses and the green stripe in your hair?"

By now all the boys had gathered around Brian in a semicircle. Toby moved in closer and said, "Yeah, you always say that sunglasses make it harder to focus on the ball."

Brian's lips curled slightly into a forced smile. "Well I decided I should give it another try, and as you can see it worked nicely."

Toby snatched the sunglasses off Brian's head and stared into his eyes. "Whoa!" Toby gasped. "Your eyes are freaky, dude. They look like my cat's."

"Oh, uh…I developed a rare eye disorder," said Brian.

Tommy interjected, "Yeah, it's called ocular retinal… nomadic catatosis."

"I've heard of that," said Dave. He caught Brian's eye and winked without anyone else noticing.

"Aw, you did not," said Roger. "Tommy's just making up

words…cat-a-tosis. Ha-ha-ha!"

"No really," said Dave. "I swear it was on the Discovery Channel last week. I think it's caused by a weakness in the retina, and it tears vertically. You know, up and down so you end up with eyes that look more like slits than dots."

Everyone but Roger nodded, as if the mention of the Discovery Channel confirmed the story.

Dave continued to roll with it. "Yeah, and some people get slits both up and down and back and forth like a star. Have you ever heard of starry eyes? Well, that is where that expression comes from. Ever hear of wide-eyed? That's a condition where your retina stretches all the way out and your pupils are like the size of quarters. But the cool part is that you can see perfectly in absolute darkness."

"Wide-eyed?" said Roger. "Now you're making stuff up. I don't believe that last part. Anyway, I would say his eyes look more like they belong on a snake than a cat."

"No, snake eyes are when the pupils are like little dots like on a dice. It's all in my dad's medical book," said Dave.

"I thought you saw it on Discovery!"

"Well, who do you think told me to watch it? Yup, my old man did!"

"Whatever," grumbled Roger. "Anyway, the game is over. That was our only ball and you're never going to find it. Brian, you owe Toby a new ball."

Brian nodded. He and the boys began strolling back to the bench to pick up their gear. "Come on, Cassie. The game's over," Brian said.

She stood, and he put his arm around her shoulders. Together they and Tommy walked away from the field. Brian glanced back to make sure they were at a safe distance from the others before he whispered, "Did you see that hit? I can't believe it!" He laughed.

Tommy practically jumped up and down. "How did you do that?"

"I was getting really irritated with that jerk Roger. I felt my chest puff up, and before I knew it, the bat felt like a toothpick."

"Are you turning into a beast?" asked Tommy.

"I don't think so. It's not like before. Like Ebil said, 'Everything in life stacks up.' I think I might always have a little beast in me, though."

"Did you win the game?" Cassie said sweetly.

Brian chuckled, and Tommy burst out laughing.

"The game got messed up, didn't it?" she said.

"Yup, it did. Have you ever seen so many people get so upset over a good hit?"

Cassie shrugged. "I have never seen any kind of hit, let alone a good one."

"Well, trust me, the hit and the reaction we got was one for the books. We didn't even get around to playing a game. We were just warming up. And, by the way, the bats we use are not the black flying screechy kind. The bat was the big stick I used to hit the ball with. I should have explained it better. I didn't anticipate it all going so badly."

Cassie laughed. "I actually thought you hit real bats!"

"What a creepy game that would be," Tommy said, still chuckling. "How many bats would you have to go through to play an entire game?"

# CHAPTER FOURTEEN

# INVITING AS A SPIDER'S WEB

LATER THAT afternoon, Brian decided to make room in the barn for the animals to stay at night, should the cloud decide to pay them another visit. As he stacked milk crates in a darkened corner, the tall barn door opened and a long angled stream of light split the shadows. Dave's gangly shape appeared out of the blinding daylight. As he approached, Brian noticed the usual smile on his face.

"Hey, Bri," Dave called. He tossed a softball up in the air and caught it.

"Dave! Hey, what's up? Oh, and I wanted to thank you for covering for me on the eye slit thing. I think the guys actually believed that you saw it on Discovery."

"Yeah, that's why I'm here. I want you to know that whatever has been going on I'm with you—okay? And as far as having eyes that look like a cat's, if it helps me get a hot girlfriend, then count me in. How did you do it? Your eyes are cool. Did you buy special contacts or something?"

Brian contemplated what he should say to his friend, not knowing where to begin. Feeling uncomfortable, Brian just said, "Nope."

"Anyway," Dave continued, "I found the ball you hit. I stuck around and looked for it after everyone left. I just had to know how far it went. To be honest, I had nothing better to do. I got a good look at the flight path as it left the field, and decided I wasn't going to leave until I found it. Well, it took me over an hour but…." He held up the ball with pride. "I got it! Then I decided to pace off the distance. I counted my strides back to home plate. Then I measured my stride, subtracted a little for going around trees and did the math. My conservative, unscientific estimate is that you hit the softball about 511 feet!"

"Over five hundred feet? That's crazy! You must have found the wrong ball. Or maybe it rolled quite a ways. A dog could have picked it up and carried it there. Look! I think I see a few teeth marks on it. Face it, there is no possible way I could have hit the ball that far. "

Dave shook his head. "No, no, sorry, I found this ball— the same exact ball you hit. I found it stuck in the crotch of tree three feet up, which is the same exact place where it landed. It didn't roll, and no dog carried it. Do you know who hits a softball that far?"

"I give up, who?"

"No one does. So my point is I am totally freaked out! What is going on with you? I was thinking that you were on steroids or something, but even that wouldn't explain it— unless they are the kind they give to elephants. You know, 'elephant-oids.'"

"No, I'm not on elephant-oids or any other kind of 'oids,' and I wouldn't touch stuff like that anyway."

Dave turned the ball in his hand and then said, "That brings me to the million-dollar questions. What's with the cat eyes? What's with the green stripe in your hair? Why do you guys always smell like dead carp? And last but not least, what's with hitting a softball like Godzilla?"

Brian smiled. "I know I can trust you, but even if I told you what's been going on you'd have to be crazy to believe any of it."

"Try me."

"Okay, fine. I spent some time recently as a reptilian, toad-faced monster, and some of its aura got mixed in with mine, like when a bee pollinates flowers. When that fathead Roger threw the pitch, I felt this surge of beastliness. I focused on that ball as if I were mad at it, made good contact, and then POW!"

Dave just stood and stared for a moment. Then he wrinkled his forehead, as if having some inner conversation with himself. Finally, he smiled and said, "It is just shocking how little of that made sense to me—but I still want in." He shrugged and then added, "Oh, I also came over to tell you that Joey is still missing.

"The latest story is that he got into an argument with his stepdad and ran off in the dark. Problem is, that was like four days ago, and fighting with his old man is nothing new for him. The neighborhood group is meeting at six to walk the woods. I guess at this point, they're looking for his body. My mom thinks some psycho-perv got him."

"What do you think?"

"That rotten kid is always up to something. He probably saw how much people talked about you and your brother, when the two of you disappeared, and he wanted some of the attention for himself."

"Are you going to help look for him? It's almost six."

"I thought I would see if you guys wanted to come with me and search. But we won't walk pointlessly through the woods like everyone else. I'm sure that jerk is just hiding out somewhere, while everyone gets all stirred up. We need to think about where he might hide, and then look there. I would love to sneak up behind him, while he is giggling, and grab him by the neck and say, 'Gotcha, you little fart-knocker!'"

Brian thought for a moment. "I know he has a thing for playing on the railroad tracks."

"Right, he gets his yucks by trapping animals and tying them to the tracks. It reminds me of this old cartoon where evil Snidely Whiplash ties Nell to the tracks because she can't pay the rent. Then Dudley Do-Right of the Mounties rides up to save the day in the last moment as the train is coming and…"

"So, you think he's just playing a trick?" asked Brian. "I'm worried that he might actually be dead. But, I do see what you're saying. We need to think like Joey. Where would he go if he were going to hide? Well, maybe it's not too late to save him before the red cloud catches him running around in the dark. I think we should try, and I have a feeling that he has something to do with the three-legged rabbit."

"Three-legged rabbit?"

"The wind told me to follow the three-legged rabbit. I think it will somehow answer all of our questions."

Dave made a face. "You hear voices, too? And what's this about a red cloud catching Joey?"

Brian sighed. "Okay. It's like this. The red cloud is very scary stuff—an evil unstoppable red blob. Trust me. It is the kind of thing that wakes you up in the middle of the night screaming for your mama."

"Whoa! Looks like I either have a lot to learn or, more likely, you guys are really losing it. Well, count me in either way."

"Okay, I think we understand each other. Come on." Brian pushed Dave toward the open barn door. Moments later they found Cassie and Tommy, who were sitting on the fence throwing grain to the chickens.

"Hey, Cassie, are you really the Flower Witch's granddaughter?" Dave asked.

"Yes," Cassie replied.

"It's all true then? Does she really cast flowers into the pond so it will take another victim?"

Cassie gave him a piercing stare and made a scary face.

"No, it is not true!" said Brian.

He turned to Cassie and Tommy and said, "Listen, Dave wants in, and I am okay with it if you guys are."

"I may be skinny, but I'm strong and quick. Oh, and I'm pretty smart," Dave said.

"What we are dealing with is dangerous, and you have nothing at stake, as far as you know. So why would you want in?" Cassie asked.

"Boredom, I guess."

"Boredom?"

"Yeah, it has been a long, hot summer. With Brian first disappearing and then ending up in a coma, I haven't had anyone interesting to hang out with. It got so bad that last week I actually watched some daytime soaps with my mom, just to see if I could sit through an entire hour. What a mistake that was. If you ever want to make time stand still, just watch daytime soaps. I am not joking—the clock did not move! If I am ever on death row and I have a final request, I will ask to watch Days of Our Lives because it will seem like an eternity before the show ends."

Cassie glanced at Brian. "Does he always talk that much?"

"He can get on a roll," said Brian.

"Of course," Dave continued, "it is a paradox, because if I were stuck watching that show I would be begging them to kill me to get it over with."

Cassie shrugged. "He is kind of entertaining to listen to."

Tommy nodded. "Okay, he's in."

"Great," said Brian. "We're going to help Dave look for Joey. If we find him, we can ask him about the rabbit's foot."

"That works, but we should bring the Miracle Mix and the cooked cloud goo," said Cassie.

"Got the crystal?" Tommy asked.

Cassie patted the lump in her pocket and nodded.

"I never know what the heck you guys are talking about, but I like it," Dave said. "What is Miracle Mix?"

"Spaghetti sauce," said Cassie.

"Confused?" asked Brian. "Well, that's great because there is plenty more you aren't going to understand. Tommy, you get the sauce. I'll get the goo. Can you think of anything else?"

Cassie said, "How about the lantern, in case it gets dark before we get back?"

Several minutes later everything was all set. "Hand me that jar of stinky cloud goo, Tom," Brian said.

Brian gave it to Dave. "Smear some of it on your neck and the top of your head."

Dave grimaced when he opened the jar. Then he spotted the jar of spaghetti sauce. "What's that for?" Dave asked. "Shouldn't we bring some noodles too?"

"That is Miracle Mix. If some red glob sticks on you, pour the sauce on it."

"Is it going to stay this weird for me, or at some point will it make sense?"

"It's still weird for us, and we know what is going on."

"Cool, I am okay with weird," Dave said, as he smeared goo into his black snarled hair.

"Don't overdo it," Brian cautioned. "That's all the goo we have, and you wouldn't believe what we'd have to go through to get more."

"Mom's going to the park to walk the woods with the

neighbors," said Tommy. "I told her we were going to look for him by the tracks. It's strange, when you think about it. We are looking for Joey—a kid who probably deserves everything that he has got himself tangled up in."

"We're doing it because it's the right thing to do. Even Joey deserves better than to be dinner for that red blob," Brian reminded him.

• • •

When they reached the tracks, the sun was still high in the sky. The blustery wind shook the tree branches and scattered dry leaves across the hot iron rails. The four of them walked the tracks, and by a little after seven, they had managed to travel a few miles out of town.

"Joey would be smart to walk down the tracks because he wouldn't leave a trail," said Dave.

"Do you really think he would put that much thought into it?" questioned Brian.

Tommy tipped back and forth as he balanced one foot in front of the other on the wrought iron rail. "Hey," he said, "there's a patch of fur right here, and a few loose ropes." He flicked the crusted skin with a stick. "Maybe this was from the bunny that lost its foot."

Tommy took the rabbit's foot out of his pocket and matched it up with the brown fur stuck to the track. "The fur matches perfectly."

"We're getting close to something, I can feel it," said Brian.

"Must have been some kind of resilient rabbit," said Tommy. "It chewed threw its ropes to get free. One paw must have still been tied to the tracks when the train went by. That is one tough bunny."

Dave was already down on all fours with his nose inches from the ground. "Hey, guys, there's a light trail of dried blood."

He crawled like a bloodhound over the second rail and into the loose gravel and weeds. "It leads that way!" He stood and pointed into the thick brush.

The sun had fallen behind the tree line, making it difficult to see beyond the outer edges of the woods. So thick was the growth, that the sun's light hit the ground in random patches. They walked cautiously toward a break in the thicket. As they approached, a brown rabbit darted from a clump of thistle. With surprising agility, it sprang ahead on three legs. Then it disappeared through the opening in the brush.

"That's our bunny!" Cassie exclaimed.

"Follow it!" Brian said, and they chased the rabbit through the thicket, but it was gone.

Once in the shadows of the trees, Brian's eyes adjusted. As they moved through the opening in the brush, he walked over a fence lying on its side. It appeared that time had eaten it halfway into the ground.

Through the trees Brian made out the shape of a small one-room house. As he continued to walk forward, the house gradually came into focus.

They stood motionless and gazed at the aged structure. It was completely obscured from the tracks. Though curious, they scanned the area quietly.

"That house is about as inviting as a spider's web," Brian whispered.

The air was rich with the smell of rotting leaves and pine needles. Thistle grew up to the bottom of the boarded windows, and leaves covered what may have been a yard. The old home was in shambles. It appeared that the forest had claimed it. Dark green ivy clung to the roof and sides of the house, spreading like an infection. Bare boards, bleached to a dull gray, formed the front of the house.

"Looks haunted," Tommy muttered, as they inched closer.

"It's totally Draculated," muttered Dave. "I bet there are enough bats in there to film a nature documentary."

"I sense something bad here," said Brian. "Even a bat wouldn't want to hang around this place."

"We're talking about the flying kind of bats this time, right?" said Cassie, peering between the splintered boards that were nailed over the window. She placed her palm on the front of the brittle sun-dried house. "Nothing is moving. It's as still as death."

Dave shuddered and said, "Still as death? You're creeping me out. Why not say still as a pond, or still as a sleeping cat?"

"Cats wake up," said Cassie. "Ponds have ripples. This place has been still and dead for a long time."

"Do you want to leave, Dave?" asked Brian.

Dave smiled and shook his head. "Leave now? Heck no, it's just getting good."

Brian stepped onto the front porch and tested its stability. The boards dipped as he stepped up to the door, but they held. The lock required a skeleton key, and the doorknob was so old that rust came off in his hand when he gave it a turn. He pulled on the knob but the door was frozen shut.

Brian turned to say something, but found that he was alone. A flash of fear ripped through him. Brian moved to the back of the house, stepping high enough to get through the prickly weeds. But when he turned the corner of the house, he sighed in relief. There stood Tommy, Cassie, and Dave peering through an open window.

Brian surveyed the back of the house. A line of weeds stretched along its side. The thick layer of leaves kept the grass only a few inches high in the yard. The door to the root cellar built under the house was shut tight—probably locked. A few feet away, an old stone well protruded from the ground. The bucket was missing, and the only evidence that the well had ever been used were the remnants of an old brown rope looped over the rim.

Dave tapped the wooden siding. "Look at the boards' discoloration." Then he pointed at the open window. "This used to be boarded up. Someone has recently opened it."

"If you give me a boost I'll go in," said Tommy.

Dave laced his fingers together, and Tommy stepped up like he was putting his foot in a stirrup. He slid through the window frame. Moments later he appeared at the window.

"It's a little dark in here," he said. "The only light coming in is through the gaps in the boards."

Brian handed Tommy the lantern and watched as his brother turned up the flame.

"Hey, someone was here!" said Tommy. "There's a sleeping bag on the floor and a knife on the fireplace hearth."

He brought the knife to the window and showed the others. "This is a butterfly knife. I saw Joey showing off with one of these once. He was flipping it around like this." Tommy tried flipping the knife so the blade would flash out, but he fumbled, and the knife fell to the floor.

"Put it back where you found it," said Brian. "We don't want anyone to know we were here."

He pulled himself onto the window ledge. Pushing his belly off the sill, he rolled into the room, like a diver rolls from a boat into the water. He noticed a small stone fireplace built into the outside wall. He watched as Tommy held his hand over the coals.

Tommy looked at Brian. "There's still heat coming off them."

Brian began a slow survey of the house's interior. A few long floorboards lay here and there. It appeared the planks had fallen from random open areas of the ceiling. The only things adorning the rooms were a few sticks and some scattered leaves.

Brian examined the sleeping bag. It had been rolled and tied neatly. "Joey is too much of a slob to take the time to roll up a sleeping bag. Whoever did this was meticulous; there is not one fold out of place. It looks like it came right from the store."

Then he spotted a splattered dark-red spot on the floor and pointed it out to Tommy.

"What is it?" Tommy asked.

Brian rubbed it between his fingers. "It's either blood or spaghetti sauce."

"Taste it," said Tommy.

"No way! What if it's blood?"

"Don't be a baby!"

Brian held it out. "You wanna taste it?"

Tommy ducked out of the way. "No!"

"How about this scenario: Maybe whoever is staying here got blood on the floor when he took the rabbit's foot from the tracks. Then he accidentally dropped the foot at our farm when he dragged Grandma Rae away."

"Sauce or blood, either way we're in the right place," said Tommy.

Dave crawled through the window and pulled Cassie in behind him. "We should look upstairs," said Dave.

"Why?" Tommy asked.

"If this were a horror movie there would be zombies or stacks of dead bodies wrapped in garbage bags, hidden up there."

"Then why would we want to go up there?"

"Good point."

Brian glanced up and noticed that access to the attic was nothing more than an open trap door with a rung ladder against the side of the wall.

"Let's take a look together," said Brian.

"Good idea—safety in numbers. Hey, see any bats?" asked Dave, eyeing the ceiling. "I've got an idea. Let's hide in the attic, and when the little creep comes back, we'll jump down and scare the crap out of him!"

"Okay, but the sleeping bag doesn't necessarily mean Joey was here," said Brian.

Brian was the first one up the ladder. When his eyes cleared the opening, he realized the attic was bare with the exception of dust and long-abandoned spider webs. He waited for the others to join him.

Cassie lay on the dusty floor and peered between the gaps in the floorboards. "This is perfect. I can see below."

"Even the dust in this place is old. There is nothing up here, and it's hotter than Hades," said Tommy.

"Just shush up and lie on the floor. We'll have to wait to see who is staying here," said Brian.

"If it's Joey, I get first dibs on jumping down to scare him," said Dave.

"It could be anyone. What if the thing that rolled up that bag took Joey or Rae? We just need to wait and watch so we can see what they're up to."

Dave positioned himself flat on the floor. "This is so cool. I feel like a cop on a stake-out!"

"Hey, Tom," said Brian. "Could you turn the lantern way down so it stays lit but isn't bright enough to give us away?"

Tommy brought the wick down to a small speck.

• • •

They waited quietly for one hour, and then two. The attic was like a dry sauna; their faces beaded with sweat. Feeling stiff, Brian rolled onto his back.

"My neck is getting sore, but at least the attic is finally starting to cool down," Dave said. "It would be just like that idiot to wimp out and go home right when we're in position to scare the stuffing out of him."

"How much longer are we going to give him? It will be dark in about an hour. I think this might be a big waste of time," Tommy complained.

"What's wrong with the dark?" asked Cassie. "I love the dark. Brian, I think we should stay. Don't you think we are close to getting to some answers?"

Brian nodded.

Dave laughed. "Cassie, you are freaky. I have to say hanging out with you guys is better than the soaps, but I'm with Tommy. I don't want to sit up here all night. I didn't even bother to tell anyone where I was going. I should go before my mom thinks some psycho-perv got me and spazzes out."

Tommy got to his feet and twisted his torso to stretch out his back muscles. "Yeah, you guys can stay if you want. Joey isn't worth this much effort. The truth is we don't know who lives here. Lots of people have knives like that, and if Joey is in trouble I don't give a cat's keister about him anyway. He deserves any mess he has gotten into."

"I think we're onto something," said Brian. "I didn't want to say anything earlier, but I sense this has something to do with the cloud."

"I know what you're saying," said Cassie. "Ever since I sank into that cloud guck, and it clogged my nose and mouth, causing me to taste it, I can sort of feel where the cloud has been. The roof of my mouth starts tingling."

"Yeah, I feel it too! The cloud has been all over this place, hasn't it? I felt it as soon as we stepped off the tracks. I'm afraid that it has eaten Joey and Grandma Rae. And if that's

Joey's knife, he may have been here at one time, but now he is gone—for good. I say we wait here. And if it's dangerous, we'll just stay put and remain quiet. Agreed? The cloud won't be able to smell us, so we will be safe."

Before anyone could reply, Brian was alerted by the sound of rustling leaves. He held his finger to his lips to warn them. "Something is walking through the woods," he whispered.

# CHAPTER FIFTEEN
# DING DONG BELL

THE RHYTHMIC shuffling noise grew louder, as whomever, or whatever, came nearer.

Brian pointed down, and they all lay flat on their bellies and peered through the missing floorboards at the room below.

The rustling sound ceased. Then they heard the sound of wood rubbing against wood and the squeal of a rusty hinge.

"Someone just opened the cellar door," whispered Dave. "We never checked it. I guess I thought it would be full of bats and giant spider webs."

They all jumped when they heard thump, thump, THUMP!

"It sounds like someone is pounding in tent stakes," said Tommy.

Suddenly a male voice started singing, "Ding dong bell, ding dong bell, kittens in the well. Who put them in? Sneaky Joey Hasselback, who strolled on down the railroad tracks, and never caused them any harm until he stole them from the farm. Ding dong bell, ding dong bell."

"I think that's Joey's voice, and by the sound of it the kid has gone loony," Brian said under his breath.

Dave stood. "Yeah, and it sounds like he's dancing! Weirdo. I knew it—I was right all along. Joey is here. I am going to scare the stuffing out of that little fart knocker!"

"Just wait a minute," Brian hissed. "Get back down and stay still. We need to see what he's doing."

He peeked between the fractured floorboards and caught a glimpse of Joey's hands grasping the window ledge. In a move of surprising strength, Joey pulled himself up and through the window with one smooth motion. He landed on his hands and feet like a bullfrog, and then leaped to a standing position with the finesse of a gymnast.

"Baby still sleeping?" Joey asked no one.

They watched in silence as Joey added a few pieces of dry wood and stoked the fire with a stick. There was a burst of flames as the logs caught. Orange embers flew like a swarm of hornets for a moment until they were abruptly sucked up the chimney.

Joey began humming. He knelt and unrolled his sleeping bag with the care and precision of a brain surgeon preparing for an operation.

Dave looked at Brian and mouthed, "Okay, now?"

Brian nodded reluctantly.

Dave stood and quietly moved toward the ladder. He rolled each foot, heal to toe without making so much as a creak. Stealthily, he worked his way down the ladder, trying his best to keep his laughter contained. With the skill of a cat burglar, he moved across the floor and snuck up right behind Joey.

Dave lifted his hands, thumped them solidly on Joey's shoulders and yelled, "Got you, you little fart…"

"Ahgh!" Joey squealed. He thrust his hand into the sleeping bag and yanked out a long twisted staff. He spun around and, with great force, banged the ball attached to the top of the staff into the side of Dave's head.

Dave's face was one of complete shock. The knob bounced off his skull and sent him crashing headlong into the dusty floor. Dave lay motionless. A small stream of blood pooled around his cheek.

Brian began to stand, but Cassie held him down. "Wait," she whispered. "Look at what he has in his hand—a staff just like Leether's. Don't charge down there until we have a plan."

"You sound like your mother," Brian grumbled. "Dave needs my help now!"

"You can help him best by waiting for the right moment."

Brian felt a chill as Joey slid two fingers around the curve of the bloodied wooden ball and then touched the blood to the tip of his tongue. "Hmm…kid eats a lot of sugar," Joey said.

Joey sat Indian style, picked up the knife, and casually flipped open the blade. He began carving small holes into the ball. He sang while rocking his head back and forth, "Ding dong bell…"

Joey let Dave lay there as if he were of no consequence. Then, after a moment, he looked at him as if he had just remembered Dave was still there. He said, "Always nosing around with your big nose. I will sacrifice you, too."

He waved the staff in a swirling motion, as if practicing. A faint red mist twirled and curled from the holes in the ball. Joey stood up in the middle of the room and spun in a circle, his staff extended. The red mist swirled from the outstretched staff.

"You feel that?" Brian whispered.

Cassie nodded and rubbed her arms.

"Ding dong bell, ding dong bell. Baby sleeps in the well,

ha-ha!" Joey turned faster.

"That's it," whispered Cassie. "Joey is the cloud's new host! We should have realized it. Leether was the cloud's host and master, but when you did away with him the cloud needed a new brain to share. It needed an evil master to help it plan and think."

"And I bet the cloud hides in the well. Who better than Joey Hasselback to accept pure evil?" whispered Brian.

"What was that?" Joey said. "Is someone here?"

Joey sniffed the air. "I don't smell anything." He glanced at the light red mist, floating out of the holes and spoke, "No. Nimbus must stay hidden until the sun is gone. It's best if people don't even know it exists. Just wait. When it gets dark we will have a sacrifice. Yes, we will go back to the farm and catch the ghost, too. I will coax them all outside this time, and Nimbus can take every one of them. It will be glorious. Justice will be done."

Joey sat back on the floor and returned to carving his staff. Soon he began to chant, "Rufescent phantom ghost-like brume, a stinging blaze, cast your haze, justice will be done for you, justice will be done. You live in the well, and Dave won't live to tell, digitty ding, dong bell."

Brian noticed a vibrato in Joey's voice that had never been there before. "He for sure is sharing his brain with the cloud," he whispered. "He's lost his marbles."

"Who is there?" Joey said, jumping to his feet. "I don't smell you but I hear you. I know you're up there and I know I will soon throw you into the well, ding dong bell." Joey picked up a board lying on the floor. He gripped the bottom of it and used it as a battering ram to bash at the ceiling. The boards began popping away from their rusty nails.

"You're up there, aren't you? Come down now or I will knock the floor out from under your feet!"

Cassie and Brian rolled toward the trap door as the boards tore loose and tumbled through the beams to the floor below. Tommy danced around and jumped across an opening. His foot struck an airborne board and, as the floor gave way, he plummeted to the floor below. He landed on his side, using his arms to shield himself from the boards raining down on his head.

Brian felt a sudden pulsating rush of adrenalin surge through his body, and he began to puff up. He dropped his legs through the trap door and hung by his hands from the rim of the small square opening. "What are you doing, Joey?"

"Brian?"

From Brian's vantage point, he could see directly through the open window and into the backyard. Shock nearly overcame him when he saw Grandma Rae staked out in the grass next to the well, her mouth gagged. It felt so wrong to see the old woman's eyes wide with fear. Brian growled and dropped firmly onto the floor.

Obviously injured, Tommy pulled himself along the floor to get as far away from Joey as he could.

Joey scowled at Tommy, and then he laughed. "Where do you think you're going, wimp? I'm not done with you yet. Paybacks are a bi…"

"If you want him, you'll have to go through me!" Brian snarled.

Joey returned his attention to Brian. "Hey, you aren't a ghost anymore. This makes it much less complicated. I can't believe that you came here. You are sooo stupid!"

Brian caught the desperate glance from Cassie as she watched from above. "Get the sauce and the lantern," he said under his breath.

"Who are you talking to? Is the black-haired girl here, too? This is too perfect—too easy. Joey smiled wickedly and started to sing, "Ding dong bell, Nimbus rises from the well." He picked up his twisted staff and raised it in the air. "Justice will be done for you. Rufescent phantom…"

"Get the staff!" Cassie screamed from above. "He is using it to summon Nimbus!"

Brian sprang toward Joey like a sprinter coming off the line. He cleared the distance in an instant and lunged forward, tackling Joey hard to the floor.

"Don't let the mist leave the staff!" Cassie yelled in panic, clambering down the ladder.

Pinned on his back, Joey continued to scream, "Ding, dong bell!" He gripped the staff tightly and tried to elevate it.

Brian glimpsed a hint of red mist beginning to once again emerge from the top of the staff.

Cassie bypassed the last several rungs of the ladder and leaped to the floor. She dropped the lantern and ran toward Brian, while simultaneously trying to unscrew the jar of sauce. Joey squirmed and grunted as he pushed with enough strength to lift Brian straight up in the air. He managed to get his knee and then his foot between himself and Brian.

"Cassie, quick hand me the jar!" Brian yelled. "I think you need to eat some sauce, Joey."

Joey kicked hard, and Brian reeled back. He caught his balance just before hitting the wall.

Cassie snarled and charged at Joey as he started to stand. Seeing her coming, he thrust the staff at her. The round knob on the end of the scepter began to emit a dark-red mist.

Cassie grabbed the knob and rammed it into the jar of sloshing sauce. A steamy red vapor gushed from the jar.

"AHHHH!" Joey screamed in agony. He pulled the staff, dripping with saucy steam, out of the jar. He winced and swung the back of the staff around, forcefully catching Cassie in the throat.

She fell away stunned and choking. But she had the presence of mind to cap most of the remaining sauce as she tumbled to the floor.

"You're killing my baby!" Joey yelled.

Brian squared off with Joey. "The cloud can't hear you, Joey. It has no ears. It's just you and me."

Joey smiled broadly. "You and me? I'm not the same old Joey!"

"I am not the same old Brian."

"You have no idea who you're messing with!"

"No, I think I have a pretty good idea. You have grown from a little pain in the butt to a big nut job."

Joey attacked, but Brian knocked him to the floor with a crushing right hand to the side of his head.

Joey stumbled to his feet and broke for the window. "Help me, Baby," he screamed.

As he jumped over Cassie, she lifted her leg and sent him sprawling across the floor. Joey scrambled on all fours toward the window. He began clawing at the window ledge. But Brian dove onto his back and hugged Joey's elbows and chest. He growled and squeezed as hard as he could.

Joey's face reddened, and he screamed.

Holding Joey tightly, Brian rolled onto his back. This forced Joey to lay face-up on Brian's chest. "Quick," he said to Cassie. "The sauce! I don't know how long I can hold him."

Meanwhile, Tommy had used a splintered board as a crutch to get to his feet. He limped over to Cassie, who handed the jar to him.

Tommy fumbled with the lid, finally got it unscrewed, and then placed it against Joey's lips. "Open up, you evil creep!"

Joey clenched his teeth together and turned his head away.

Tommy pushed his thumb into the back of Joey's jawbone. Joey's teeth unclenched slightly, and Tommy was able to force some of the sauce inside Joey's mouth.

Joey tasted it. Then he threw back his head in pain and screamed.

Seizing the opportunity, Tommy poured in more sauce. The sauce overflowed and spilled from the corners of his mouth.

"Ahhghg!" Joey yelled, flailing about as if being burned alive.

Brian held on with all his strength while Joey kicked and squirmed. "Swallow," yelled Brian. "Swallow!"

Tommy squeezed Joey's cheeks together and kept his hand over Joey's mouth.

Then Brian felt Joey's esophagus contract as he gulped a mouthful of the sauce.

Joey's body writhed with pain, and then went limp. Brian released his grip, and Joey collapsed to the floor. His body began to tremble, as if he were having a seizure. Then he suddenly stopped moving, and his pinkish skin began to wash out into a dull shade of gray.

"We didn't kill him, did we?" asked Brian. "I didn't want to kill him! I couldn't let him get to the well and wake the cloud."

"We had to do it," said Tommy.

Cassie rubbed her throat and crawled over toward Joey. She put her hand on his cheek. "He's cold." Then she gasped. "Look! Look at his nose!"

Red gelatinous goo began exiting from both nostrils and ears. It was faint and pinkish, at first, and then, in moments, became darker and thicker.

"Oh my gosh, that was inside him!" she exclaimed. "He was following in Leether's footsteps."

The red ooze rose off him and began forming into a small balloon-size cloud overhead.

"If that cloud makes it out the window, its game over," said Brian. "The goo is like a carrier pigeon. It will go to the well, where Nimbus is sleeping, and wake it up!"

From the other side of the room came a groan. Still lying where he had landed, when Joey knocked him out, Dave tried to lift his head. His face was bloodied, and he was missing two front teeth.

"Stay still," Brian told him.

Dave's eyes rolled back, and he passed out again.

"Remember," Cassie said, "we have the cloud goo on us. The cloud can't smell us, so it can't see us."

"That's right. Maybe now is the only chance we'll ever have to kill it!"

"We could pour the sauce into the well, but we don't have enough left to do the job."

"I'll make the well a flaming hole," Brian said, as he glanced at the lantern.

The small gooey cloud wavered for a moment, and then disappeared through the window.

"Wait, you can't just throw the lantern into the well," Cassie said. "The fire will go out when it hits the water."

Then Brian smiled. "I know how you like plans, and I have a good one."

He cradled the lantern and threw his leg over the window ledge. He looked back. "Be ready to hide everyone if this doesn't work!"

Jumping from the window, Brian saw the last glint of red goo dive into the well and disappear.

Brian ran by Rae, who was still tied to the ground. Her mouth was gagged but her eyes were screaming.

"Rae, hang on!" he yelled.

He unscrewed the fuel cap on the base of the lantern. Moving quickly around the well he coated the inside wall

219

with the lantern fluid.

"What are you doing?" Tommy called out from the window.

"When that fat cloud squeezes out, it will get coated in lantern oil. Then I will light it up!"

He heard a loud rumble from deep beneath the ground followed by a mighty thunderclap. BOOM! A hot rush of moist air wafted up.

Suddenly, Brian felt a cold flood of despair wash over him. "I used up all the lantern oil, so the flame went out!" he cried in utter frustration.

The cloud suddenly erupted from the well, scraping the wall with its mass. It formed into a gigantic blob over his head.

"Fire! I need fire to light it up!" he yelled.

Cassie disappeared from the window, and seconds later reappeared with a burning stick from the fireplace. Despite the obvious heat from the burning wood she held fast. She wound up and sent the hot branch spinning through the air toward Brian.

It landed in the grass, just in front of him. He lunged for it and snatched it from the ground. The flames continued to flicker, and the stick glowed red. "Come here," he growled. "Come and get me!"

He rocked his arm back, preparing to launch the flaming torch into Nimbus. Lightning flashed from within the cloud, and it erupted with a sudden drenching downpour.

Shocked, Brian watched the bristling flame turn into nothing more than a smoking stick. "Oh, no!" yelled Cassie. "The goo will wash off you. Run! It will be able to smell you!"

Brian froze for a moment. Then he made a mad dash for the house. But before he could reach it, he felt the weight of the icy glob smash him into the ground and knock the wind out of his chest. Completely encased in the numbing goo, the blob, still connected to the cloud, lifted him into the air. As he rose higher, he could make out Cassie and the old house through the thick layer of gelatinous orange goo.

He realized Leether had accomplished his goal. He was stunned and in utter disbelief that it was going to end like this. Despite the odds, he never believed, even for a moment, that the cloud would get the best of him.

He kicked and fought but he could not move from its thick gelatinous grip. He began to feel numb all over. His aura began to separate from his body. He wrapped his ghostly arms around his helpless body and tugged and pulled but could not break his body completely free.

Wracked with despair at the hopelessness of the moment, his spirits lifted when he saw Cassie. She appeared orange and blurry from within the blob. She was taking something out of her pocket. He saw the twinkle of the glassy crystal.

Cassie reached back and snapped the crystal forward hard. The crystal sent a crackle of white-hot electricity deep into the cloud's mass.

A flash of yellow and then red blazed around him as the entire cloud became engulfed in flames. He felt the very fabric of the cloud breaking up. The tremendous heat threatened to overwhelm him.

Then he was falling back to earth, still lodged in a massive ball of flaming goo. Brian struck the ground, with the goo taking much of the impact. He lay numb and dumbfounded as his aura locked firmly back into his human form.

Fiery fragments of the cloud fell to the ground and ignited small areas of dried leaves. The still-drenched ground from the earlier downpour kept the fires from spreading. Lethargically, he wiped the hot gelatinous goo from his eyes. He caught sight of a smoke trail streaking across the sky—

the remnants of the cloud burning as it fled.

Brian lifted his head slightly. His first sight was of Cassie throwing herself on the ground beside him. She clasped his face in her hands, and wiped the steaming glob from his cheeks. "I love you, Brian!" she said, hugging him. "There is no one else like you!"

Brian smiled groggily. "I love you, too, Cassie. And trust me; there is no one else like you either!"

Brian shook his head to clear his vision just in time to see Tommy help Dave half climb, half fall out of the window.

Tommy pumped his fist in the air and yelled, "We did it! We did it!" Then he noticed Grandma Rae still staked to the ground and limped to her as fast as he could. He pulled the gag from her mouth and released her from her bonds. She gave him a huge, tearful hug, once she was able to sit up.

"Oh my!" said a confused Grandma Rae, as she unconsciously began brushing the dry leaves from her dress.

Dave put an arm on Tommy's shoulder and together they hobbled toward Brian and Cassie.

Brian heard the snap of a twig and quickly turned to see that Joey had also jumped from the window. He stood with the jar of sauce in one hand and the staff in the other, a look of astonishment on his face. "What is going on?" He licked the sauce from the corner of his mouth. "Mm."

"What do you remember?" Brian called.

"I remember that you are an idiot," he answered.

Brian smiled and sat up straight, with Cassie still wrapped around him. "I think you are going to be just fine."

"I'm not hanging around with you jerks," he said. "I'm going," He staggered a little and then regained his balance, steadying himself against a tree with his shoulder. "How did I get here?"

"Drink a little more sauce, Joey; you might feel better."

Joey looked at Brian and disdainfully tossed the partially full jar onto the leafy ground. He looked at the twisted staff in his other hand as if he had never seen it before. The fact that he was even holding it seemed to surprise him. "Is this your cane?" he asked.

"Yeah, it is mine. Give it back!"

Brian ducked as the staff sailed inches over his head.

"I'm going home," Joey said. "I feel weird. I don't even remember what day it is."

Cassie helped Brian to his feet, while holding onto his arms. "It's all over now," she said. "We did it, and I feel great!"

"Are you sure you're okay?" he asked.

"I burned a few fingers in the fire, and I have a sore neck. But it was so worth it! Actually, I feel fantastic!"

She hugged Brian again—this time hard and secure.

How content he felt at that moment. The cloud had been sent burning across the sky, and his cheek was pressed against Cassie's shiny black hair.

Then to Brian's dismay, over Cassie's shoulder, he saw a hint of something else in the sky. It was just a speck at first. But then it grew steadily clearer. There was a small winding trail of smoke coming back toward them. He felt the roof of his mouth tingle. "It's coming back!"

"What?"

"What's left of the cloud is coming back!"

"It must have gone to the pond to put out the fire, and now it's coming back for us!"

"I've got this," said Brian. He picked up the staff and held it in the air. "Rufescent phantom, cast your maze and blue. Cat's in the cradle and a ding dong bell um…"

"Oh, my gosh! What are you doing?" Cassie said in a panic.

"I'm calling that disgusting thing in. We can still finish it off. When it gets close you, sauce-ify it!"

Cassie scooped some of the spilled sauce back into the jar—dirt, grass, and all. She stood ready. "Try to get it to enter the ball; then we can stick it inside the jar."

As the cloud grew closer, Brian saw it was now only the size of a smoking grapefruit. The smoking goo cleared the roof of the house and swooped down at them like a hawk closing in on a rabbit.

Brian raised the staff and chanted, "Ding dong bell, ding dong bell, get in the staff and I'll melt you."

"Make it rhyme," Cassie pleaded. "I think it is supposed to rhyme."

"Oh! Um, ding dong bell, you came up from the well, and the farmer's in the dell." He held the staff high in the air and the cloud went for it.

He moved his head back as the cloud came directly at him. It went right past the staff and pushed its entire mass up Brian's nostrils.

"AHHHH!" Brian yelled, his eyes bulging.

Cassie screamed. "It is making you the new host! Hold still, hold still!" She pushed the jar up to his mouth and poured in the sauce. "Don't swallow until I say so."

Brian's cheeks bulged.

"Quick, cover your ears," she yelled.

"Huh?" Brian mumbled, his mouth full.

"I said cover your ears!"

Brian slapped his palms against his ears while Cassie shook the remaining sauce from the jar. She jammed her shirttail into the jar and quickly wiped out the remaining residue. Brian trembled as the goo began to emerge from his nostrils. Then Cassie reached up and pinched down as hard as she could on his nose to keep the goo inside him.

Brian groaned in pain.

"Keep your mouth shut," she warned. Nudging his left hand off his ear, she pushed the jar firmly against the side of his head. "Now swallow," she said.

Brian blankly looked up at her.

"I said swallow!"

Brian took a big gulp. Like a thick worm, the red goo shot out of Brian's ear and into the empty jar.

She quickly tipped the jar up and spun the lid, screwing it down tightly.

Inches from Brian's face, she looked into his eyes. "Is it all out? Is that it?"

Brian nodded.

"Got it!" she cried. "This time we got it!" She danced around holding the jar over her head.

Brian staggered and grinned. "Yessssss! That was quick thinking. Whew! Game over! Your mom would be so proud of you." He took the jar and held it over his head.

"Yeah, I bet she would," said Cassie. "Woo-hoo! Justice will be done for us."

"YAAAY!" He shook the cloud in the jar. "No justice for you! No, never—not ever!"

"You guys are amazing," said Dave. He looked happy, which was in direct contrast to his missing teeth and bloodied face.

"You did it!" said Tommy "It is all over."

"Are you guys gonna be all right?" Brian asked.

"Nothing that can't be fixed by my dentist," said Dave.

"Don't change a thing," said Brian. "The toothless thing is kind of a good look for you."

Dave smiled back at him.

"My leg is messed up," Tommy said. "But I don't think it's broken."

Rae came up behind them carrying a soft brown rabbit in her arms. "The bunny—it came right up to me," she said.

In elation, Cassie hooked arms with her and they began to dance a clumsy kind of do-si-do.

Brian did a funny jumping jig, while shaking up the remaining blob trapped in the jar. He felt Cassie put her hands on his waist, and he turned to look at her.

"Are you okay?" she asked.

Brian breathed in deeply. "My sinuses never felt clearer. Yeah, I'm alright!"

Cassie bounced with excitement. "This is what we were meant to do. If you didn't have the strength of the beast, and Rae didn't make great sauce, none of it would have worked."

"And if you hadn't recovered the crystal, I would be dead, and the cloud would have eaten the whole world," said Brian.

Cassie beamed. "There is no one else like you."

"Or you," Brian said with a grin.

# ABOUT THE AUTHOR

DAVID STRICKLEN'S 22 years as the Chief of Police for the Gerald R. Ford International Airport in Grand Rapids, Michigan, gave him a sense of adventure and problem-solving skills that he's used to give his writing authenticity, blade-sharp action, and believability. Having two grown sons, with whom he has greatly enjoyed a myriad of escapades, has also added flavor and color to his stories.

Recently David has become a favorite guest presenter in his community's schools, sharing his experience as an author and teaching students the creative process of writing a story. He also spends time assisting former law enforcement associates with special security projects, and volunteering at Gilda's Club. Biking on the trails and roads of West Michigan with Dan Sharp, illustrator for this book, and spending time with family are among his favorite leisure time activities.

David believes that the second book in a series should take the reader to the next level. Through the Eyes of the Beast does just that. It is a towering tale in the Blackwater Pond series, built upon the framework of the first book, Beneath and Beyond.

David and his wife Cheryl live in Grand Rapids, Michigan, close to their children: Justin and his wife Kelsey, and Jordan.

FOR MORE INFORMATION ABOUT THE BOOKS
AND AUTHOR VISITS,
## VISIT WWW.BLACKWATERPOND.COM